press.

a novel.

by franklet.

"Oh God
Could it be the weather
Oh God
Why am I here
If love isn't forever
And it's not the weather
Hand me my leather"

—*from "Leather" by Tori Amos*

"No one likes an ugly boy with self-esteem." - Alex

for Jane.

Press by franklet

2nd Paperback Edition

Revised Edition, 2017

Ray

East 14th St., New York, NY

"To exert steady weight of force against; bear down on."

Ray squeezed the fat on his arm just above the armpit. He squinted into the mirror, hoping to change the shape of it in his mind. It was Tuesday. He was already late. But that wasn't in the front of his brain. His neurons fired instead on the off-kilter shape in the mirror. Bulges and curves. Strange dimples in stranger places. They only led Ray to get hung up on the meaning of being a man.

Is this it?

He grabbed his crotch and frowned, tucked his piece further between his legs. Grunting with masculine dissatisfaction, Ray picked up his comb and pushed back his long hair, smoothed it. Tried not to fixate further upon his flabby arms or drooping moobs. His hand made the back and forth motion with the comb, so familiar, so customary, and yet in that moment as disgusting as if he had left shit stains on his panties. When he finished with the comb, Ray used the same plastic length to gently shape his mustache—a sprawling thing which curled gently around the corners of his mouth like graying brown parentheses. Ray took one last look at himself, shirtless in the full length mirror. Crafted a face, he would not have been able to describe the look, but it held a fierceness about it, a cloudy Sunday anxiety.

He put on a loose-fitting polyester blouse. The row of pearlesque buttons on the right were round and shiny, the material shiny and sleek, although cheap. Ray adored the color and glisten of the fabric and buttons, it made him feel warm, comfortable. The long sleeves of the cream-colored shirt had a single button sewn on each cuff. Ray had to resist his workman's urge to unbutton those cuffs, to roll them up. He noted his trimmed fingernails, which had been filed smooth the day before yet were still a quarter of an inch longer than his fingertips. The glossy glimmer reflected back a fuzzy, diminutive image of Ray's face, blurred into some unrecognizable blob of variegated shadow and light.

Ray turned to look at himself again in the full-length mirror hanging from the door of his closet. He usually kept that closet closed—not wanting to risk the possibility of its contents being seen—but tonight it was open. The door with the mirror was slid several feet along its brass track from where it normally reflected the solid black bedspread and linens of Ray's bed. He twisted his broad shoulders to the side —admired his figure, the flabby curves—searched out well-known flaws, like cataloging old friends who had died and left him with only obligations. With a jerk of his head, Ray's eyes drew out perspective, took in his whole shape, wholly accumulating it into one distinct form.

It made him smile. The S-class swerve of his body amid

6

the twist—if only he could exist in that pose long enough to be *truly* seen. Untwisting, Ray picked up the last piece of his outfit, pulled the skirt over his hips, and slid the zipper up. The snugness around his hips, the luxuriated slick of the silk and squeeze of the fabric delighted. The skirt flared just above his knees into a ruffle and Ray shook his hip, imitated the wind moving it, swooshed by the sound of pride itself in his imagination.

Sitting down on the edge of his bed, Ray put on his pale white shoes. He wasn't sure they were appropriate—but they flashed sparkle, made the most satisfying *clack-clack* when he danced across his kitchen floor late at night. His shaved legs were bare and as he secured the shoe on his left foot, he ran his hand delicately up his leg, sighed at the firmness of his smooth calf. *No lumpy fat there!* Ray wondered at the risibility of nature, to put such a glorious shape in a place so infrequently noted. But Ray knew nature had a vast and inexhaustibly wry sense of humor. His life was a constant reminder.

Shoes in place, Ray stood, allowed himself one more twisted moment to admire the pageantry in the mirror. Knowing more might lead to yet another outfit change, cause him to be later than he already was. He was not terribly daunted by the prospect of being late. In fact, he was mildly amused at the rightness of tradition his lateness would imply.

No. Don't want to be like my ex-wife...

Adding hurry to his steps, Ray attached accessories and walked closer to the mirrored closet door, pressed his face almost against the glass as he examined his makeup. He was never sure how much was *too* much, but the idea of having too *little* was a decidedly more frightening possibility.

Final checks of his zippers, heels, and nails done, Ray attached dangly earrings. Clip-ons. He hoped Pauline would not have a negative opinion of clip-ons. He had not been able to bring himself to pierce his ears yet. If the date went well, maybe he would have the nerve to consider it. Actually leaving the apartment fully and correctly dressed was enough of a Herculean effort. Earrings were the proverbial last bird to land on the teetering car, plunging it into the crevasse of the unknown. But that was getting too far ahead of himself. Grabbing the little clutch purse, the one with gold detailing matching the thin belt around his skirt, Ray gave an exhalation of joy. A long drawn out anti-sigh, the rush letting the air out of his anxiety. Regardless of how the night went, he could return to this moment. To when the smoothness of his calf slid gently against the silky fabric of his skirt, when the ruffles made their warm swoosh, countered by the clack of his heels as he descended the stairs of his 14th street apartment building. No matter how much his life seemed wrong—to be literally wrong, the weight of it synonymous with undesired, unnecessary masculinity—in this moment, this presage of a life not truly his, he could always swim in lightness. An airy quality he was sure must be the province of princesses.

The cab ride was not long, he didn't live far from the restaurant, but it was not a pleasant experience. It never was. The anxiety he might be recognized always warred with the voice his mind, the voice which *wanted* recognition. Demanded it, even as it rejected the possibility. The voice always sounded like his only son's, tone and diction so eerie and similar. Ray often pictured the words hovering in a speech bubble next to Alex's mouth. Such a moment always brought a hangover sadness. The thought of how long he had gone without seeing Alex, without hearing his voice, however simulated, always made Ray feel worse. Added to the worry the cabbie might recognize him... Ray dispelled the thought, rubbed his calf up and down for relief, liking the silky, muscular smoothness.

The cab trundled along. Ray resisted the urge to yell out directions to the blurry Arab. To offer a better, faster, more efficient route. Still he was afraid such a comment might mark Ray himself out as a fellow cabbie, arouse unwanted suspicion. *I'm not ready for that.* Instead he looked out the window, shocked when his heart caught sight of someone, did a flip-turn inside his chest.

"Stop the cab!" he barked. The cab screeched to a halt, jerked Ray's face forward across the glass of the window, leaving a smear of beige along the slick surface. Ray ignored this, fished out some wadded up bills from his clutch purse and threw them at the driver. He vaulted himself out of the cab, white high-heeled shoes first and his heel caught on a dimple in the asphalt of the curb, nearly tripping him. Ray caught himself on the door of the cab at the last moment. Looking at his long-sleeve covered arm, he saw a black smudge where it had rubbed hard against the gasket of the door.

Is everything going to rub off tonight?

Ray bit back a snarl of profanity, slammed the door shut just before the cab sped off down Seventh Avenue. Ray jogged across the street—careful in heels—towards the figure now half a block distant. Normally, Ray would feel self-conscious running, dressed so. Running was *not* part of the fussily crafted image of his frilled fantasies, and unladylike to boot. Long strands of blonde-gray hair streamed behind him, as did the white fabric of his skirt—the ruffles in front waved beautifully—it was not wholly unpleasant as he caught sight of himself in a mirrored window, though unexpected. The figure was steps ahead now and walking slowly—seemingly without purpose. Ray caught up as the figure stopped for a quick look into the window of a gay porn shop, one of many which lined 8th Avenue in Chelsea.

Ray caught up, reached out his arm, and laid his hand on the man's shoulder. That shoulder was bared and muscular, the other man wore only a white tank-top above a pair of khaki shorts and flip-flops.

"Davis?" Ray said, tone questioning, though he had no doubt this man was exactly who Ray expected him to be. The man froze, whipped around. A frightened snarl lit the man's face until he took in the whole of Ray's appearance. It was not the reaction Ray would have liked, a quick moment of confused revulsion, overcome by shock, and pursed, angry lips. Sudden, hard recognition dawned.

"Mr. Richardson?" Davis said, eyes darting about, trying to

take in again the whole of Ray Richardson, who stood pearlescent and blowsy before him. A mustachioed puzzle whose first piece was indistinguishable from its last.

Ray nodded to the young man, pleased Davis remembered him, despite all the changes. He had not seen Davis since before Alex disappeared.

"So... how, um, are you, Davis?" Ray asked, not ready to ask the question he most wanted to ask... not yet at least.

"Er... *I'm* fine. I didn't know you, er, lived here? I thought..." Davis said, stumbling over his words, Davis's eyes trying to keep his mouth from blurting out that Ray was wearing women's clothes.

As if I don't know?

Ray took Davis in. The last time he had seen the boy, now a man, he was a wisp of a nineteen year old. All bones and energy, racing around Ray's house at two in the morning for some purpose Ray never understood. Ray had known *why* Davis was there. He had not believed, as Cathy had, that Alex and Davis were *just friends.* And that was before Ray had unwittingly spied on his son and Davis having sex. The gawky, pieced-together Davis was gone. In his place was a muscular, thick-limbed man; with bulging biceps and a chest which looked like slabs of plate armor affixed above Davis's slim waist.

Steroids?

Ray had read about it in a magazine once. That and something called HGH, which apparently killed some of the women who took it. Otherwise he might have been tempted to try it himself. Ray saw the discomfort he caused Davis. Unasked questions blooming like visible lesions on Davis's skull: painful and jarring. "I just moved here a while back," Ray said. He wanted to say more, but his tongue stuck to the roof of his mouth, unwilling.

Davis looked confused, gathered himself, and said, "I didn't know... are you going to a... costume party or something? Um, where's Miss Cathy?"

Ray sighed. He had moved far from Denham Springs, Louisiana precisely to avoid questions about Cathy. But questions always came, as if Fate was determined to prove Ray's prior life had not been punishment enough. That he would forever have to answer for the lies, misdirection, and lack of empathy was something Ray truly believed.

"No, not a costume party. I have a date tonight. I've decided to stop denying who I am, Davis. I am a bisexual cross-dresser." The relief which came every time he said the words aloud was similar to the exhalation of joy he felt at the sound of rustling silk, the delicate squish of fabrics on his bare skin, the clack of his feet walking in heels. There was something magical to the confessional nature of it—Ray imagined it becoming addictive—but what happened when you ran out of people to shock? Davis was certainly shocked, if the look on his face were evidence.

"Well... I..." Davis stuttered.

"Cathy is in Denham Springs. We've divorced. It's not what I wanted, but she couldn't accept this. *Me.*" Ray gestured over the whole of his shimmering body. Davis nodded.

12

"So. How's Alex?" Davis asked, hesitant. There was a note of obvious desire there. Ray had been having a hard time adjusting to understanding those signals in the eyes and on the faces of other men, had often wondered about his own expressions, had they been the same? Ray started to chew his lip—making his mustache hop like a furtive mammal, an old habit.

Lipstick!

Ray stopped gnawing, hopefully before he smudged his lips or got lipstick on his teeth. Being late was bad enough, he didn't want to be unmade as well.

"I had hoped... when I saw you..." Ray said. He really had hoped Davis would have seen Alex, would know where Alex was, vain as such hope must be.

Like everything else hope offers.

"*I* haven't seen Alex in years, Mr. Richardson. I don't even know where he lives anymore. Why don't *you* know?" Davis asked. Ray shouldn't have been surprised to find Davis and Alex no longer spoke. It had been ten years since their relationship ended and they had been each other's first loves, an acrimonious setup in the best of situations. Ray had refused to endorse their relationship—had wanted, publicly, to know as little of it as possible—once Cathy had told him it was a fact.

So many regrets.

Ray nodded. "Well, if you see him, could you..." But even as he spoke, he saw the crestfallen look on Davis's face, knew the man did not like him, even now. Exposed, new. Alex must have shared with Davis, must have told him about Ray's attitudes and beliefs. Told him—likely in bed, wrapped in one another's arms—about the horrible things Ray had said to Alex time and again. How could Ray tell anyone, least of all Davis, how much those words had hurt Ray himself? How those words had been meant for his own heart, misdirected by life's cruel intentions to be aimed instead at his son's? How seeing a face so like his own—decades younger—on a *gay* son, so strong and sure. How it had both inspired and terrified a father with a secret fear so strong it should have its own fairy tale hero with which to prattle? Ray had recited that futile argument many times. He knew it was no use. He had made so many mistakes and they hurt, but he *had* to live with those mistakes, and would have to die with them. There would be no respite from the likes of men like Davis, nor Ray's own regrets.

"Sure, Mr. Richardson, I'll tell him I saw you," Davis said wavering. Lying. His face was now easy to read. Didn't the man remember Ray had been a police officer before? A homicide detective learned how to see the lies on people's faces, after twenty-eight years on the force.

He doesn't ever expect to see Alex again. But he wants to.

Ray remembered playing the lying game with Davis and Alex—when Alex had first brought the boy home for dinner—before Ray had known about Alex being gay. It had amused Alex to show Ray off, such an infrequent occurrence Ray had always been happy to oblige, plussed by the attention. Did Davis remember? Apparently not.

14

"Well. Thanks, Davis." Ray had more to say as he extended then pulled back his hand for a shake, Davis was already edging away. How could Ray fault him for it?

"It was nice to see you Davis, really. Good luck," Ray said. Davis smiled, even as he backed off. Ray saw why Alex had loved the man: his off-kilter smile was devilish and beguiling, his ever so slightly not-straight teeth had a pattern as pleasing —moreso to Ray—as a row of bright, whiter teeth. The man was pebbly and handsome in an off-hand manner, his boyishness now a faint shadow. Davis waved, uncomfortable and brusque, turned away, now moving faster than before Ray had stopped him.

Ray caught sight of the smudge on his sleeve as he held his arm up to hail a cab. It was frustrating trying to keep oneself so *clean* all the time. So perpetually shiny. How had Cathy managed all those years? How had he never noticed her effort? Ray missed being allowed to be arbitrarily messy, even as he was glad he was not any longer.

Climbing into the cab which stopped in front of him, Ray gave the Paki driver directions: "57th and Fifth, please."

A digital clock hanging from the rear-view mirror of the cab read 7:51. *I'm to be more than a half-hour late. Hopefully, Pauline will wait.* Ray would hate to end up back home, alone. On a Tuesday night with an opened closet of silky clothes and the two sides of himself, which seemed at those lonely times so irreconcilable.

15

Davis

Seventh Ave. Greenwich Village. New York City.

"To extract by squeezing or compressing."

"I. Hate. This." Davis said into his iPhone through drawn lips and clenched teeth. Seventh Avenue was clogged with faggots. Cookie-cutter queens slummed in from Chelsea, sometimes in pairs, sometimes alone. When in pairs they often had mirror-image biceps and color-matched outfits. Tank-tops exactly the same (except one was red the other blue) above the same Banana Republic cargo pants and expensive sandals or flops. Davis found it revolting. Most were by themselves or in groups larger than two, but the pairs always made Davis angriest.

Hadn't he done everything he could? Taken fucking steroids TWICE? And now he *had* the body and the mind. Was smart enough to bury these pretentious assholes physically and intellectually. Yet they *still* didn't look at him. *Is it my teeth? And Mr. Richardson, and WHAT the FUCK was that?* Seeing the man after ten years, in fucking drag which was at least thirty years out of date, was almost too much. That frizzy, long, blond hair and a fucking moustache, a FUCKING MOUSTACHE?

In the first scattered moments Davis had been sure it was a joke. When he had recognized the man — for a brief second — something flared inside Davis. A hope he had thought long gone, vanished along with the childish feelings he'd once had for Alex Richardson. The sad hope that the strange moment somehow *was* Alex reaching out for Davis, through his dragged-out father, as astronomically unlikely as that would be, struck him as terribly ridiculous. Davis had not spoken directly to Alex in eight years. Not counting brief sightings on Scruff, Facebook, Grindr, and Craigslist—all while Davis had been still new to Manhattan. Even then, it had taken some sincere effort to see the Alex Davis had once known in the pictures of the buff, confident, dashing man in those profiles and pictures. *Had Alex done steroids also?* Davis had thought.

How could he *not* think of Alex now? Despite the awful way Mr. Richardson had treated Alex, in one of life's most ass-fucking ironies, the man turned out at be a faggot himself? *That* was rich. Davis remembered the pattern from memory. Alex seeing the disapproval in Mr. Richardson's face. Disapproval aimed at Alex, not for his choices, but for something he innately *was*. That had led Alex right off the cliff. And to think it was just Mr. Richardson expressing his *own* self-hatred the whole time. Mind-boggling.

Maybe when he got home he'd look again for Alex online. Just to see how he was. Nothing else. There wasn't any lingering feeling there. Just curiosity about a first love, long past. That was natural wasn't it? Davis sighed and slowed down. He looked back, relieved to see no further sign of Mr. Richardson following. Davis remembered then he was still in the middle of a conversation on his iPhone.

What had Jules been saying?

"Ack. Sorry Jules. I zoned. What's going on?" Davis said.

"Nothing, Davy. Just talking about this guy I've been seeing. Prather. Can't figure him out. He's Indian. Claims he's an artist, but when I started talking about paints and colors he frowned, said I was thinking like an ubermensch. Whatever *that* is. Do you know what that is? Cuz I don't. Wanna go see that new movie? The one with that guy with the nice man-V who dances, can't remember his name... it's like Stockard or something. Davis?"

Davis blinked. Studied his reflection in the window of a sex-toy and porn video shop. "Channing. Channing Tatum, Jules. Not Stockard Channing. That's a woman," Davis corrected her. Jules snickered into the phone.

"Yeah well, I figured *you'd* know. So what d'ya say? Wanna come with?" Jules' voice was the same high-pitched squeal it had been since the first time Davis met her—not surprising once you saw her—she was an inch under five feet tall, small-framed to boot—like an elf lost inside a rave for a few years who came out PLURed to insanity. She was his best friend. Had been since senior year of high school. She had agreed to move to New York with him three years before—although they hadn't lasted long in the same apartment. Jules was *not* easy to live with.

"Not tonight, Jules. I just... I don't know how to even say this." It's what he had meant earlier when he'd said, "I. Hate. This." The feeling he was *missing* something, but having *no* idea what the something was. Like those times when he told himself to remember something and two days later all he

18

could remember was he had told himself to remember *something*, but never the actual thing he needed to remember. Jules brushed his comment aside.

"Don't know how to say what, Davy?" Jules asked, tone showing concern. He was still *her* best friend.

"I just saw Alex Richardson's dad. Remember him? Mr. Richardson?" Davis said.

"OH MY GOD! You mean *the* Alex Richardson? Wait? What? His Dad? Where? I thought you were window shopping in the Village, I mean how?"

"I dunno, Jules. But he was *here* and that's *not* the kicker. The man was in *drag*. He *came out* to me! Said, and I quote, 'I'm a bisexual cross-dresser now, Davis.' Can you fucking believe *that*?" Davis barked. A really young faggot—with a shock of platinum blond hair and the super-slim figure of a longtime meth addict—sidled out of the sex shop Davis had been peering into. The kid smiled ravishingly at Davis. Davis *knew* that smile, his dick got hard when he saw it. Not that he knew the kid—just another faceless twink faggot—but the expression said the twink was high and ready to fuck. DTF to the straight people. Davis adjusted his crotch and smiled back.

"Davis? Are you still THERE? You can't be SERIOUS?" Jules screamed into the phone.

"Yeah, um, I gotta bail Jules... just remembered something I need to... handle. Sorry 'bout the movie. Just not up for it tonight, maybe tomorrow? Talk to you then." Davis hung up the phone without waiting for Jules to reply.

"Sup," he said to the twink faggot.

"Sup," the boy said.

"Davis," Davis said, grinning.

"Anton." He beamed crookedly and checked Davis out. Bright blue eyes drinking in the sight of Davis's muscular frame. Those fucking Chelsea queens might not look at him, but boys like this did—like catching dick-hungry fish in a barrel. Alex had looked at him like that once, all the time in fact, but that was before Davis had gotten ripped. Before the steroids and HGH. When Davis himself had looked disturbingly similar to the twink faggot before him, only taller, with dark hair and eyes.

"So," Davis said, returning the smile. "Wanna go somewhere?" Promising everything he could with just a smile. He loved these fucking methed-out twinks. At least for a night. A few hours. A weekend. They were useless otherwise. But the things they would let you *do* to them. So appalling and yet so... compelling.

"You party?" Anton asked.

"Nah, but I've got supplies if you need," Davis offered. You needed bait if you were going fishing.

"Sweet. Yeah, let's go, you got a place?" Anton said hungrily.

Great. Another homeless hustler thinking he's found a place to stay for the week. I'll fuck him regardless. Even for a week. Davis thought about how much meth he had left. He had no intention of going over to Pritchard's again so soon for more. He might be able to stretch the boy's need over until early next week, with effort. But that depended on what the boy let

20

Davis do. If his promise paid off.

Davis returned the hungry stare. "Yeah, it's just up in Chelsea. Let's go get some poppers and we'll catch a cab. Cool?"

Anton nodded and relaxed. Like something vital had seeped out of him. The extraction itself a form of pleasure. Anton reached over to grab Davis's hand and squeezed it, made a puppy dog face of affection, far too loving for Davis's desire to violate the kid. Davis looked away and sighed, thinking about Mr. Richardson and, sadly, of Alex.

Anton

8th Avenue, Chelsea, New York City

"To make compact by squeezing or compressing."

Is he looking at me?

Every time he turned a corner of an aisle of soft-core cheese porn, Anton looked up at one of the men littering the place. He didn't know the name of the store, had never bothered to look or remember if he had. What did it matter after all? Anton had instead learned to recognize hook-up spots by the window displays. The conspicuous highlighting of sex toys, lubes, and leather gear—not some stupid innuendo-laced title flashing tacky on an awning above a plate glass storefront.

None of the men seemed to be looking at Anton. It was like that sometimes, and Anton knew it. You could be beautiful to a great number of men—if never all. Your whole person could exude the definition of archetype, you could be the literal meaning of twink, and still feel unnoticed. Anton remembered the first time someone had called him "the archetype of a twink." Part of him had *wanted* to be offended. Because he hadn't known what "archetype" meant. Being labeled a twink made him feel useless. Full of an anxiety he could hardly define—like the whole of his life would someday become voided by the word *twink*. As if he would look back some day to the moment, when he had first been called a twink, and see it was *the* seminal moment. The first shot in a war lost before it began. But Anton didn't think this way. He never went beyond base emotions, instead he just felt anxious about whether or not he was being cruised.

Years before, after looking up the word "archetype," Anton had been pleased, at first. He had stuck upon a word in the definition: "model." Dwelt on it. Anton had wondered if that's what the guy had meant when he called him the "archetype of a twink." That Anton should be a model. Anton then embraced the twink label to a large degree, at times even reveling in it. Taking joy in being young, thin, and handsome —but in no way overwhelming. It had suited him in almost every environment over the four years since the first time he had heard the word "archetype."

Yet he could hardly remember the man who had called him "the archetype of a twink." Only that he had met him in a sex club on 27th street, when Anton was fifteen. It had been one of Anton's first forays into the sex club scene in Manhattan. Not his *very* first. There had been trips to the Manhole and the East Side Club. But Anton had always thought of those as training grounds. He had looked and sucked, but hadn't let anyone touch his dick, or his ass. It was the club on 27th—*what was its name these days?*—where he had met the Archetype Guy.

Anton shook his head trying to recall the club's name, but could not snatch it from memory. He had never been good with names and this one, unlike the others, was clandestine. Under the table and secretive. In all likelihood, he might never have heard about the club on 27th—with its innocuous name

Anton couldn't recall—much less made it in, if he hadn't been trolling the very sex shop he was currently in. Looking for a hookup and some tina. A small, note-card-sized flier between two fisting porn cases had led Anton to the sex club on 27th street.

At first the club was scary. The freakiness of the stuff which went on there: the fisting, the monstrous toys, the slings and nipple piercings. But Anton had gotten swept up in it all. Gotten so high he could barely walk. He discovered what the cliché of being a kid in a candy store *truly* felt like—only he was both kid and candy at the club on 27th. Those men had *used* him. Introduced him to the very *notion* of being used. To an exquisite depth of the word. Pumped him full of drugs; more poppers and more Crisco. Shown him an ecstasy so primal and vibrant that the next time Anton saw daylight he was unsure if he had actually lived through the experience. Or if instead he had died and been reborn as something revolting and new, stumbling down 27th street towards 8th avenue, his ass leaking lube and need. With *that* guy. The one who had called him the "archetype of a twink." Whose name Anton still couldn't recall, if he had ever actually been told what it was. The Sunday morning sunlight had been horrid and bright. Washing everything in shadows and orangish glows. It had confused Anton. Made him wonder: *is THIS heaven?* Wandering through light and shadow. Floating in thrumming, soft-dick, open-ass fugue. His ass a point of rhythmic pleasure which beat in time with his drugged heart.

It made sense at the time.

Anton spent some time with *that* guy after *that* night at the club. Maybe a week, maybe a little more. He had never been sure quite how much. They did *things*. Anton was resistant at first. More drugs calmed him into it. After a few days, it felt like he had been doing *those* things his whole life. As if nothing felt quite *right* without doing them.

The guy was older. But not much. Early twenties, late twenties as most. Tall, thick but not fat, handsome but not especially so, *comfortable*. His apartment was nice, not large. Anton remembered the funny carpets in vibrant colors: swags of bright yellow, blue, and pink; and *action figures* on the bookshelves alongside toys from the 1980's: CareBears, Transformers, She-Ra, Ninja Turtles, Garbage Pail Kids. But those were small, insignificant details in the larger picture of sex and drugs.

Anton and the stranger did things which made fisting and toys feel *tame*. Things which Anton still found himself embarrassed to so thoroughly enjoy. Embarrassed to ask for until he got high, at which point he would beg. Never secure enough to be the first to reveal. Eventually, the drugs ran out and the guy made Anton leave.

Anton's parents hadn't been happy he had disappeared for days with no word. He had done it before, if never for so long. But they were wealthy *artists* who lived in a communal loft in DUMBO, too busy expressing the *ineffable* (whatever that meant) to take constant note of Anton's presence or lack thereof. Between smoking K2 and taking research chemicals like 2C-B and occasionally selling a piece of grossly overpriced shit some morons generously called art, his parents might find time for him. When Anton reappeared after days gone, told his parents he had been "busy figuring out his sexual destiny," they had hugged him, offered rapt expressions of commiseration. Told him that was *so important* —how *proud* they were. But next time could he just try and let them know he was alive after a few days or something? Because they had worried their drug dealer *sick*. Pestering questions about whether or not the dealer—Trevie—had seen Anton around, fully aware of their little Anton's sexual dalliances with Trevie.

"Trevie got SO mad at us!" Anton's mom had almost shrieked. As if Anton hadn't bought drugs from Trevie since he was *eleven*. Sucking the dealer's ass since he was thirteen. The admonition of Trevie's anger had been the end of whatever parental concern Anton's parents had shown for his days-long disappearance.

Never one to sit still for long periods, Anton had again grown restless. His mind had constantly, consistently, and uncontrollably gone back to the club on 27th street. To *that* guy's apartment. Even back then, he had forgotten the guy's name. Anton thought maybe it started with an A, like Anton's own.

Regardless, Anton never saw the guy again. He'd gone back to the club on 27th four or five more times. Until the city finally shut it down and it moved elsewhere. Anton never found it again. Instead, he started frequenting sex shops— looking for note-card invitations again. Hoping to get lucky

26

and *get lucky.*

Get high. Get laid. Get used.

Wandering back from that night—from around that first time he'd been called a twink—Anton's mind flitted back into the present. To the leather-vested, young muscle-daddy shopping through piss porn. The man occasionally looking over at Anton as he shuffled fisting porn cases; occasionally reading the back of one until he realized he had already seen it several times. Anton was still looking for an invitation hidden among them. But every time Anton tried to catch the guy's eyes, flash some spark of lust, the guy looked nervously away.

For fuck's sake, is he looking at me? Probably not. Probably wants a bear or someone older.

Anton sighed. His will steeled, his ass thrummed, and he decided it was time to flat out ask the guy if he wanted to go somewhere and party. Need trumped hesitation. He walked over to the guy, watched the thickly-muscled man as he swallowed hard and fled out the front door, like a frightened hen. Anton sighed again.

He may not have technically been jailbait anymore, but Anton certainly *looked* the part. No one ever believed him when he confessed to them what kind of sex he wanted. What he really liked to do and who he liked to do it with.

"You're too young!"

"No way, that's disgusting! But you're so cute, why do you want *that*?"

"Man, I'd totally do that to you if you were for real..."

Most of those guys—the hot, hairy, older guys—they wanted someone older than Anton. Someone with facial hair, someone with chest hair. And the purists, they wanted someone older and someone clean, not a twink who wanted meth along with his perversions.

As if. Who needs to be pure to get shit on?

It was rare Anton found a man into twinks like himself. The man was usually a *poseur* of a daddy, the kind who just wanted to spank Anton, listen to him endlessly say, "More, Daddy!" and whine like a little bitch. Not that Anton was opposed to that—his little dick would shiver at the deep throated slur of a hairy man calling him a bitch, commanding him to beg for his pleasures—but *that* was the beginning of foreplay. Not the main event. Never enough to satisfy. But *those* guys—those *poser* daddies—they never wanted to go as far as Anton wanted.

Ready to give up on the sex shop's prospects, half-lost in his memories, Anton moved towards the door, determined to go down to the next place—the one with the huge dildo that cost like four hundred dollars. The dildo Anton fantasized about having a Daddy *force* him to sit on. Going there and seeing what was up, hoping maybe he'd meet a hot daddy there. He started to shake, jonesing for some tina, or even better, a whole eight ball of it. To smoke up into a fever pitch of anticipation at the sex he was eventually *going* to have. He rarely got everything he really wanted, but he always got laid. Being a twink ensured at least that much. And if everything else failed, he could always hang out on St. Mark's at Astor

Place until a straight guy, slumming, took him for a hustler. Those guys would sometimes do what Anton wanted, and sometimes they'd *pay* him. And their asses were always dirty. But the last time Anton had tried, he had nearly been arrested and that terrified him.

As he was nearing the door to the sex shop, Anton heard a whispered, "Psst..." and he turned around to see where it had come from.

Oh shit I forgot this place has a backroom.

Anton walked over towards the nondescript door, the door people who didn't know better would take for a mere storeroom entrance. He pushed it open and walked in. Eyes adjusting to the darkness, ears to the volume of the thumping music, the sounds of men grunting.

"Sup," a deep voice said. Anton blinked, trying to see the guy's face. The guy wasn't young. That was good. Already Anton saw he was fat, not muscled. Not a deal-breaker—but not inspiring either.

"What you into?" the voice asked.

Anton saw the Daddy more clearly now. Early fifties maybe. Balding, with a salt-and-pepper beard and a slight paunch above a flabby lower body encased in a pair of black khakis below a rumpled, grey polo. Definitely not Anton's type, quite beside the fact he already had his dick out and it was smaller than Anton's. Unless the guy had tina, he was shit out of luck as far as Anton was concerned.

And not the good kind of shit *out of luck.*

"You partyin'?" Anton asked—not bothering with

29

answering the man's question until he determined whether or
not there was tina to be had. Anton saw the confused look on
the man's face and his spirits dropped. He knew *that* look. The
bearded man was trying to understand what Anton meant by
partying. Which meant he had no idea. And certainly had no
tina. Annoyed, Anton decided to cut further to the quick, take
a chance: "Drugs, man. Tina. *Crystal meth.*"

The man's face dropped and he looked pissed. "Nah. Not
into it. Wanna just suck this dick?" He waggled the pathetic
little thing at Anton. Anton grimaced and said: "As if."

He walked out of the backroom. Didn't bother looking
around the shop again—already determined to go elsewhere.
That's when he saw through the storefront windows: a tall,
well-muscled, young Chelsea queen, chatting on an iPhone.
Wearing jeans so tight Anton could see the impression of the
guy's cock-ring.

Cock-ring.

Score.

Rushing, Anton hurried to the door and out. Put on his
most pathetically alluring smile, a hang-dog expression of
neediness, the one that guys like this Chelsea queen always
ate up.

"Sup," Anton said as the man hung up his iPhone with a
comment to which Anton paid little attention.

The man said, "Sup."

"I'm Anton."

The rest happened very fast.

A few hours later Anton rolled over onto his stomach,

lowered his legs. The guy—David or Travis or something—went to go get them some food. Anton wasn't hungry—not for food—but they had to eat if they were going to keep doing what they had been doing for the past two hours.

Not to mention the meth.

Anton had learned: in order to stay *truly* fucked up, you *needed* to eat food—replenish your body's stores. Keep the hormones flowing. Heedless of the semi-damp, quickly crusting mess covering most of his chest and face, Anton reached over to the night stand, grabbed the glass pipe, and carefully filled the bowl with a good-sized shard, making sure to use his mostly clean hand to insert the meth. Shit didn't burn well, even if it gave Anton a high to eat it. Shivering in anticipation of the hit, Anton grabbed the torch lighter and burned the bottom of the bowl, exhaling first to blow off the cut. There wasn't much. This guy had great tina. Anton took steady, pulling breaths until he was spinning and floating. Pausing only for a bit—and doing it again until the bowl was empty. When he was done, Anton rolled over twice in the king-sized bed until he was again on his stomach. The bed was covered by a thick, rubber sheet. This guy—Travis or whatever—had *serious* money to afford rubber sheets, Anton knew. They cost hundreds of dollars. The material was slick with sweat, grease, piss, cum and little mounds of shit.

Occasionally Anton would look up at the porn still playing on the flat screen hanging in front of the bed. It was a porn Anton had never seen. The porn was pretty hot, even though what the six guys were doing was nothing new to Anton,

31

except for the fact they were doing it to what looked like a little kid, maybe thirteen or fourteen years old. Shaggy-haired, with crooked teeth and pointed hip-bones, like some 70's teen icon.

Anton figured it out quick after that: Travis was into little boys. After all, Anton himself *looked* like one. But Anton had to smoke almost a half a gram of tina before he felt comfortable enough to start asking the leading questions to get Travis—or was it David?—into a discussion about what Anton needed. It had taken surprisingly few questions. Aside from being an aspiring pedophile, the guy was a pervert with few, if any, limits. Once he was sure Anton was serious, that Anton really wanted that kind of humiliation, he'd offered to shoot Anton up, something Anton had never done. Anton agreed, without hesitation. Things got crazy after that.

He was still feeling the effects of that shot of tina coursing through his small frame when Anton developed the chemical courage to beg for what he wanted. The liberation which came —so fierce and unexpected—seconds after the needle pierced his inner elbow was more than Anton could have described. His vocabulary was far too stunted for such transcendence. After he stopped coughing, he had bluntly asked, formed words that seemed etched like grooves into his soul, a melody played by the needle.

"Do you have to shit? I wanna eat it. I want your shit all over me."

The guy blinked, shocked by the question. They had only talked so far about pissing, fisting, and light domination. The kind of things Anton thought of as "gateway sex." But then Travis—David?—shit, it could even be something like *Chris* for Christ sake. Names were so easily shed. What was the point of learning them for just a night or two? A weekend? Anton had gotten by for a whole week once only calling a trick, "Dude."

He never saw the slap coming. The muscular man's open hand crashed across Anton's face like a diagnosis of cancer of the ass. The man snarled at Anton, "You fucking cunt slut."

Minutes later Anton lay on his stomach, snorting and grunting into a pile of warm shit. Alternately nuzzling and grinning at nothing, like a pedophile Santa Claus. It was glorious. He hardly felt the hard slaps to his ass or the fist which punched him in the ribs before slamming deep into his guts. All that had happened before the guy, whose name turned out to be Davis, had left to get food.

Replenishment for the brown-eyed monster.

That's what Davis had said to Anton, who had lain on the floor with the sullen but pleased expression of a bored teenager routinely pressing buttons on a video game, who happened to be covered in drying, rapidly crusting filth. A moment of inspiration would strike Anton and he'd noodle around the rubber sheet, scoop up some tiny amount of leftovers and slowly lick it off his finger.

By the time Davis returned with the off-white plastic bags full of food, Anton had devoured most of the shit which had caked his own body. Rather meticulously licked most of the rubber sheet clean. His smile had nuggets of brown in it, but

33

he was unaware, bouncing up and down on a massive sex toy as thick around as a two liter bottle of soda. He purred at the sight of Davis, sweat-slick under his tank top and shorts, the smell of his body odor spiky and acrid, even over the earthy shit-reek wafting around the room. Davis was younger than the usual cut of man Anton levered into abusing him, but his body was crazy hot: hairy and muscular, thick and slab-like everywhere. *Definitely worth it.*

Most guys he played with often said they did not get high, but the moment Anton smoked up, they would as well. Not Davis though. He was animated in his repulsion of the drugs, frowning and slanting off disapproving glares every time Anton paused to draw on the meth pipe. The man's features made it seem he was unaware of the nascent disapproval on his face. But Davis wasn't frowning now. The sight of Anton's sprightly frame bouncing up and down on a fencepost-like toy with a slightly bored, but still rapt, expression was obviously turning Davis on. Davis set the plastic bags down and pulled out the contents: peanut butter jars, chocolate bars, dried fruits, bread and marshmallows. Davis studied Anton with an earnest gaze, causing Anton to hover with his ass full yet inches off the floor, like a dog considering its master's desires. Had Anton been sober, he would have recognized the look on Davis's face: the "unicorn" look.

It said, "You're the most amazing, freakiest, nastiest and SEXIEST piece of filth I've ever seen and I want to own you forever. And I hope you like me, too."

But Anton was too far gone into the realm of prurience,

34

too focused on the ripples of pleasure radiating up and out from his ass and gurgling shit-filled stomach, from the buzzing insouciance of the meth high.

Davis's question was so strange when it came in that moment as to have a quality of surrealism. It did more than rhyme with being a shit-stuffed unicorn with an ass full of rainbow heaven. "Why do you *hate* yourself so much?" Davis asked.

Anton blinked and slipped, fell on his side. The toy inside him slipped out and slid across the slick rubber sheet. Fell to the floor with a prophetic thud. Anton's ass puckered and whined, letting out silent puffs of previously trapped air, like hipster huffs of disappointment. He tossed his face up at Davis and tried to form words, paused to think harder, only to eventually force the word "What?" out.

"I mean, it's cool." Davis said. "I'm into it. I like you like this. But how *old* are you? Sixteen? Seventeen? You're so fucking pretty and so fucking sexy... your *body is perfect*... and yet you love men to desecrate it. You *get off on it.* Why?

"Why do you want men to do this shit to you?"

Davis's tone was clear: he was curious. He wanted to *understand* his unicorn. Anton never thought of himself as a smart boy, but he knew his prey, knew them well. Yet in all his playing, no one had ever asked Anton these questions. It nearly pulled him out of his high, but he managed to hold on to that, if only by an eyelash. He all but lost sensation in his ass, the huge toy which had felt like a missing part of him sitting unwanted on the floor, like a crack baby. He glared at press >franklet

Travis, David, Davis, whatever, unaware he was doing so.

"I..." Anton stuttered, worrying at the question, worrying more about his answer. He had rarely thought about *why* he did what he did. Maybe it was *that guy's* fault—the one from the club on 27th, the guy whose name he could never remember despite trying—for showing Anton how soul-curing it could feel to be used and abused by another man, showing Anton that sexual humiliation had been what he always wanted. What he had always needed; and never known. Until then. But even sober, Anton could not have articulated that understanding, that need, to Davis. Nor could he have detailed much of the source, as he couldn't even remember the name of the man who first debased him. Unsure how to answer, Anton fell back into the same kind of manipulative lies he frequently used on men he intended to dash on. Often stealing their tina and cash before he fled, still caked in their shit in places under his clothes—while they were in the bathroom washing off their guilt or something.

"Because you're so hot... I dunno. I just feel like I need you to use me. Like maybe I deserve for you to use me. Like I exist for *you* to use and humiliate me." Of course, Anton had said things exactly like that before, parroting back some of the lines various men had thrown at him. His lies had usually been of that ilk: flattery mixed with deprecation, petty manipulations he used without planning them out, because they always worked.

The unicorn effect.

Anton would not have described it in that way, his

36

thoughts were too simple. *I like men to use me. I feel special when they become nasty enough to give me what I need. What I deserve, for being a faggot whore. When I know it's something about me twisting them into dominating me.*

"Whatever." Davis's narrowed his eyes, as if the answer were transparent, as if he saw it for the lie it was. Before Davis could respond, Anton fired back, the words spilling out, the question unplanned.

"Why do you like fucking little kids? Why do you like doing *this* stuff to them?"

Travis, David, whatever, looked offended, angry. "I'm *not* into little kids. That's a *midget...*" Anton's head swung towards the TV, and now that Travis had said so, he saw it—it *was* a midget in the porn. The little person's whole body plastered with shit. Anton sighed and swallowed hard, sure he was going to get thrown out soon, unsure what to say next to prevent it.

"I like abusing twinks because they always get all the attention. Because no one notices gay guys after they are twenty-one. Unless they look like you or a Chelsea muscle queen or something. But mostly I just like seeing how far I can push a guy, what his limits are. Then convincing him to go further, watching the lust behind his eyes drown out his self and be replaced with worship. Worship for me, for what I've shown him."

Anton shifted and picked up the massive sex toy, bored with the conversation. Confused, no idea how to respond. "Got any more poppers?" Anton said, trying to change the subject.

David, Travis, whatever his name was, nodded. Got up, went to a little fridge in the corner, pulled a fresh bottle of Jungle Juice poppers out of the little freezer and handed the cold glass container to Anton, after pulling off the plastic seal first.

It was only then, after Anton took a few hits—David had pulled the huge toy away from him, was busy trying to slip both of his hands simultaneously inside Anton—that Anton noticed the photograph on the nightstand and immediately recognized both the man behind him and the man from the sex club on 27th street. Arms wrapped around one another in the photo; faces youthful and full of that particular kind of gleam which said there was love between them. Anton's eyes bulged from the feeling of his ass being stretched open as Travis plunged both forearms inside him, but also from the unexpected sight of the man who had introduced him, so long ago, to all this stuff.

Anton was far too gone, in too primal a state, to ask Travis, David, Davis, whatever, whom the guy in the photo was. But part of him noted and recorded the picture. Hoped when he sobered up, if he was still in the guy's place, that he would remember to ask the guy in the photo's name; and *maybe*, somehow, get his phone number.

Jules

8th Avenue, Chelsea, New York City

"To iron, as clothing."

Jules hung up the phone, shook her head as she tried to call up an accurate image of Alex Richardson's father in drag, still bearing that obnoxious police-issue mustache. The thing had always looked like a dead squirrel hovering above the man's thin upper lip. *What a freak!*

She put her iPhone on the desk, in front of her monitor, glanced up to make sure no one had messaged her on Facebook or OKCupid. Nothing had changed in the minutes she had been halfway on the phone with Davis.

Men suck.

She wondered at times what the deal with Davis was. Not that she was in love with him anymore; she had been once and was honest enough to admit it to herself, and to him. Mostly when she drank a lot of wine. But really, that phase had passed. Now, though she valued Davis as her best friend, at times the friendship felt one-sided. Like she was the only one talking, the only one of the two who cared. Like one hand clapping. Davis still called her sometimes, sent the odd text or message on FB, posted something amusing on her Timeline. They hung out at least once a month or so—but even then, she'd watch him get bored in real time. His mind so often flitting off elsewhere until he would steadily get more and more disinterested in being around her. Become antsy and fidgeting. Until he finally made some excuse he thought her too stupid to see through. Then he would leave.

Likely to go have fucking sex with some other asshole faggot he had met on an app. On fucking Grindr or Scruff or whatever the gays were using at the moment. Or at a video store or something. Davis had explained all these venues to her and she still had trouble accepting the reality of it. Gay men had the sex equivalent of an outlet mall available twenty-four-seven; all-you-can-eat ass shopping. In Manhattan, no less.

Years before, when they had moved to New York City together, Jules fancied that she and Davis told each other everything. Held nothing back. And god fucking knows she had told him her darkest secrets. About Jonny and his games when they were little kids. About the two abortions within six months when she was sixteen. And about the fucking Bad Seed—whose name she still wouldn't think of, much less say aloud—whom she had nearly driven herself crazy trying to please. Quitting the best job she had ever had. Alienating her family and most of her friends in the process. Jules even told Davis why she had done all that for the Bad Seed, something she had never told another living soul. But while he told her things—mostly about Alex, with some kinky sex stuff thrown in (though again mostly about Alex)—nothing he told her, now she looked back on it all, had been *truly* significant.

It was like Davis held on to *that* stuff—unaware of the

point of mutual sharing between best friends.

Sighing, Jules got up from the chair in front of her computer desk—tried to push thoughts of Davis out of her mind. After all, didn't she have real, important stuff to worry about?

Like Prather?

They had had the most amazing fuck-sesh two nights before. On a threadbare mattress covered by a ratty sheet—in the loft where Prather lived. With all those deodorant-refusing, dreadlocked white hippies and artistically motivated hipsters. Despite her distaste for the location, the sex had been *ah-mazing*. Jules got warm every time she re-imagined it. Prather had done things to her she *never* thought she would feel, at least not without being on ecstasy. And his cock had been the perfect size—not too long and just thick enough—she had cum so many times she had stopped counting.

Yet her warm feeling ignored part of what had happened: as soon as she stopped cumming, Prather had flown off her and over to the other side of the room. It was not really a room, just a space cordoned off by hanging sheets inside the loft of an old warehouse somewhere in Brooklyn. *He fucked me, then started PAINTING!* Like Jules had no longer even been there. She coughed, tried to get his attention. When that had not worked, Jules called out his name from the bed. When that also did not work, she wrapped herself in the ratty sheet, tried ridiculously hard not to think about what else might be on it. Walked over to stand behind Prather, careful not to let her bare feet step on the plethora of paint trays, bottles of water

41

with brushes in them, or stacks of canvas, some painted, some not; or the ash tray with the half smoked joint they had lit up earlier. All of which was scattered about the place, unordered, itching at Jules.

How can people stand that?

Just before she reached him, Prather turned around. But not as if he had heard her. It was like he had forgotten her completely. Only when he turned around for some other reason, only then had he seen her and remembered she was there. Wrapped in his nasty fucking sheet, standing amid his artistic detritus, wanting his attention. He nodded at her, smiled a watercolor smile at her.

That smile. Had she ever seen another like it? Gentle and evocative, giving more of an impression, a stain of pleasant implication, than any smile had a right to offer. His teeth were mostly straight, but the canines were turned just slightly outward, and for some reason Jules loved that. The teeth themselves were not white—not really—more like the dull, off-white of a coffee drinker, a lifetime smoker, both of which had resonated with her in a way she did not expect.

Those teeth had complimented his light brown skin in a way she could not readily describe. They just *fit*. She had smiled back and tried to sidle up closer to him, maybe talk to him about his art. Men loved that shit. As soon as the words left her lips she recalled that she did not know what she was talking about. Maybe Prather had guessed that. Still, it was no reason to insult her, calling her a nebbish. She didn't know what that meant. Had to look it up on Google a few hours after. It was a Yiddish word—*was he part Jewish?*—that meant *ineffectual and timid.*

He *looked* Indian, maybe Pakistani. Jules had not been bold enough to ask. But when she had seen what nebbish meant, she had almost wanted to vomit.

Weak? Ineffectual? What the fuck?

Since then, he had not answered any of her calls, emails, texts, or tweets. Had not responded to her friend request on Facebook. Hadn't posted anything new to his Instagram feed.

I mean REALLY, what the FUCK? How do guys do stuff like that?

Worse, Jules was not even sure he had cum while fucking her. *Was it the sex? Did I somehow disappoint him? Did he think I was too ballsy?* Guys sometimes told Jules they felt intimidated by her, implying she was too dominant.

As fucking if! And he thinks I'm ineffectual?

She debated calling him again. Giving him a piece of her mind. Even if it was only to his voicemail. Being forceful and hard instead of trying to sound disinterested while she practically begged him to *please just call me back.* Or she could go see that movie, the one with Stockard Tatum in it, the hot dancer guy.

Jules yawned, covered her mouth with her hand. It was early for shit's sake. Too early to go to bed, even for a Tuesday. Besides if she did not smooth out these crazy fucking thoughts, if she didn't find a way to understand—manufacture a fucking catharsis—she would wake up in the middle of the night to self-brutalize. To probably cry and eat

43

so many fucking Michelina's boxed dinners she would be shitting manicotti for a week.

A Michelina's doesn't sound too bad right now.

Jules was halfway to the kitchen—already mentally running through a catalog of frozen dinners in the fridge—when her phone buzzed from the bedroom, where she had left it sitting on the computer desk. Quickly pushing aside thoughts of chicken nuggets or fettuccine Alfredo, she ran back to the bedroom, nearly tripped over the computer chair before she managed to grab the iPhone and swipe it open. She almost dropped the phone when she saw the caller ID.

Prather, no last name. Just Prather and the 212 phone number.

What the shit is that?

Very little about Prather had been normal or mundane. It was definitely something she liked about him. He must have been in New York City a long time to have a 212 cell phone number.

"Hel...lo?" she said, trying not to sound too excited or too unexcited, or desperate, or like she had been waiting or not waiting—and failed. The last syllable squeaked out violently.

"Jules." Prather said, voice deep and resonant, calm and measured, so confident and sexy. "I misplaced my phone, Jules. I get lost painting sometimes," he paused, "But I finally checked my email this afternoon and saw you sent a few." She was glad he couldn't see her because her face went crimson remembering the seven or eight long-winded emails she had sent. None of it had been angry or demanding—not really—

44

but she *had* felt pushy. *What is the point of holding back?*

Fucking ineffectual my ass.

"Yeah," was all she managed to get out. Prather didn't laugh or sigh, just said, "OK. Hold on for a second OK?"

She said, "OK," but it sounded like air forced through a pinched tube. She listened as he had a quick conversation with someone named Tat-yee or something. Jules heard about searching, something about drugs, and eight days or maybe eighteen. It was hard to hear detail over the occasional sounds of low jungle music coming from Prather's end of the call. The conversation finally ended with Prather saying he would make some calls and see what he could learn.

"Jules, I'm sorry but I have to go. But I was hoping to see you again. Soon. Are you free tonight?" Prather asked.

Jules hadn't realized she was holding her breath until she exhaled hard into the phone, it must have sounded like a grunt on his end.

Or a fart.

She went red with embarrassment. Thank god this shit was not on FaceTime or something.

"Um. I was going to go see a movie with Davis, but he's probably going to cancel anyway, so yeah, I'm free. What did you have in mind?" Jules said, breathless.

"I don't have anything in mind yet, and I don't have time to figure it out at the moment, I've got something important to handle. Have to help one of my housemates with something. How about we meet at Union Square, outside the Virgin Records, say eleven PM?" Prather said.

Jules thrummed with excitement and belated disappointment at him so blatantly telling her he had something more important to do first.

What the fuck? Is it too much to ask to BE the most important thing to SOMEONE. For ONCE?

Men were all the same. Gay, straight, bisexual, whatever. They really just had *no clue.* Still Jules was careful not to let any of that come through in her voice. "Yeah, eleven is OK. I'll see you then?" Jules said, still sounding oddly hesitant to herself. And a little choked, despite her best efforts.

"Great. See you then, Jules," Prather said, and the line went immediately dead.

Jules set her phone down and went to her closet. Flipping through the outfits for something she would not have to iron. She was supposed to *like* ironing. The Bad Seed had told her that once while she complained as she ironed his shirt for work. The dickshit was a fucking waiter and still had never understood being crisp meant more tips. Especially at the upscale place he somehow managed to work at, despite being barely functional. Jules had done her share of waiting tables and even managed a restaurant—an Applebee's to be sure—but still, it had given her perspective. She hadn't been sparing in pointing that out to the Bad Seed. And before the Bad Seed, Jules *had* enjoyed ironing for others. For herself, somewhat less. Ironing for others had always given her a sense satisfaction. Like what she imagined being a mother must feel like, only far less involved. After the Bad Seed dropped her though, nothing—especially ironing—had felt the same. Like

46

doing it at all meant she was agreeing with *him*, even though she had believed it before he ever said it. Before she had ever known he existed. That hadn't made her changing feel any less like a betrayal of self. Like she had been doing it for him, enjoying it simply because that asshole had told her she should.

It had been like that with other things also. The vacuum tracks in the carpet which used to bring her such orderly peace of mind. The perfectly organized freezer. And the socks, rolled just so. Jules refused to do any of these things anymore. In a way still protesting *him*—though the Bad Seed was years in the past.

At times, Jules wondered if she would ever be able to escape her past. Cut free of the things idiot men had done to her, the Bad Seed only the most horrible of a long list. How much of herself would she alter? Smooth out, flatten to the point it became acceptable again, until they saw her for what they *should* see her as? Until they valued her for what she was truly worth? Shaking her head to dispel such thoughts, Jules thumbed through her closet's contents, searching for something to wear, determined, whatever it was, not to iron it.

Prather

DUMBO, Brooklyn, New York City

"To clasp or embrace closely."

The sound of paint hitting the canvas was lurid. Sexual.
Slop. Thunk. Drip.
In fact, sometimes it actually gave Prather an erection, one he would then be unable to dispel. Until he could prize out the very root of the stimulus; his mind would just hover in neutral, waiting. Finally, relentless with need, Prather would find something to fuck; so he could *just paint* again.

That the fucking was incidental, a mere human need and never an art, was nothing anyone ever wanted to hear. So Prather never bothered to tell them. Not anymore. He had tried to explain some few times, but it was like digging with a fork in wet sand. The only thing achieved was confirmation—to Prather himself—*words are never going to be my forte.*

Paint and color. Those are my lusts. The sex is just a band-aid. An ointment.

Prather had wished for so long to find someone who felt the same vitality in art. He never wanted to think of this person as a possible soul-mate. That sounded far too much like involving god or being in a soap opera. But the rushing displacement of the reality around him, when it swirled in colors behind his eyes and coalesced into a shaped need, a pulse of energy which raced down the nape of his neck, spitting itself out with a vehemence onto the canvas; he had so often hoped to share *that* with someone, had been disappointed so many times he had stopped searching. He would laugh when people talked about finding the *one*. It was the same laugh, neither derisive nor sarcastic, but sincere—as if he finally got the joke, even though he had not ever actually been let in on it. That same laugh he would give when other artists he knew talked about being married to their art.

Pretentious shits.

Of course, Prather didn't feel *that* way. His art was like an ex-wife, a pair of former lovers who shared well-loved children between them. But married to his art? In *love* with it? *Never. There should always be turbulence, rage, and unmet need in the art.*

What was love anyway? Chemically induced vagary that always led to the same inevitable, rote situation. Love had nothing on *art.*

True art is always new, different, and sublime.

How can you have the tempestuousness necessary for real art, for soul-wrenching beauty in something as mundane, as lock-step as a "marriage," even a metaphoric one? If that were the case, Prather might as well paint well-lit cottages with snowbound eaves. Or tastefully deceitful Americana landscapes, for people who needed god more than they needed taste or an appreciation of art.

Prather slashed his arms toward the canvas again, drenched the painting in a broad splash of pink so pale you could only make it out as pink when it was layered over the few splotches of black dotting the canvas. The painting had neared its apotheosis, its last moment of womb-like comfort in darkness quickly fading into the light of finality, its path now set. Two more slashes and a series of s-like strokes, and Prather stepped away. Moved back to take in the whole. The thoughts in his mind resonated with the painting, the colors a mixture of what looked like green; baby's vomit dappled with a trail of bright, azure droplets. *When did I do that?* More than anything, more than the feeling strumming in color-shifting flashes inside him, the forgetting told him the painting was *done*. It was time to cease the embrace. Push the parasite away. Free the beast; give it to the world. Prather knew: *when a painting has become mysterious—even to me—when parts of the work seem alien enough... when I can no longer remember when I made them, or how, or why...* Then the work was done. The art had finished being a part of him, was now *something else* entirely. Needed to be cut loose before it drained him completely. Still, he feared the cutting more than anything.

His erection had not left him. Looking down at it, splatters of paint decorating the shaft in places—there was paint drying on his balls even—Prather blinked in confusion. *How did I paint with an erection?* It had never worked that way before. Had he reached some new level of understanding, some higher place in his relationship—*not marriage!*—with the art?

Confused, Prather gave his dick a few exploratory tugs, closing his eyes to see what images his mind would call up. Perhaps the images, the urge, would point him in the direction he needed to go to satisfy himself. That usually worked. When painting wasn't involved. Flowing, blurring pictures flitted by—graceful men, large-breasted women, a Rothko—none of it clarified or specific, fuzzy with ambiguity. Letting his mind continue, it finally settled on an image.

A wholly unexpected one.

That woman—the amazing one. Prather had forgotten her as soon as he had closed the door on her, gone full in on the art, so there was nothing left for anything else. Somewhere he had stored her name—recorded ineffable details about her to use later in a painting. Something dark, desperate, clingy, and hovering on the edge of psychotic.

Jules.

Now why did she float into my mind?

Nothing about their encounter had been original for Prather: the sex was mediocre at best, he hadn't been able to cum even though she had, but he had fucked her until his body lost interest. Until even dreaming of paint or canvas no longer jolted the blood into his junk. He was sure she was still cumming when he pulled out of her. That had been a nice feeling—one he was not sure he had ever had prior—so perhaps there *was* something original about her—maybe that's why she was floating around his mind now while he delicately played with himself.

Her curvy form (wrapped in that old sheet of Anton's, the formerly black one which had been grey so long Prather didn't think anyone else knew what its original color had been) undulated in Prather's imagination, and he felt himself nearing climax. Pulling his hand away from himself, his eyes flashed open with inspiration. He looked around for his phone. It took some time to find, he rarely kept the thing turned on or easily available: *how could he paint with such a foul distraction?* He paused while the thing turned on, only questioning for a moment if he was doing the right thing. He had good reasons for not wanting to see Jules again, even if he couldn't remember what they were, having forgotten most of the details about her. Likely if he thought about it long enough he would recall, but he'd still need satisfaction, and most of the other girls would only present problems of a different shade, a tint of unpleasant circumstance. The guys were a different matter entirely, a satisfaction so unlike the women, Prather at times objected to the fact both experiences could be contained by the same, short, unsatisfactory word: *sex.* Surely those experiences deserved their own words, their own special significance.

The phone finally turned on and Prather shopped through the numbers, looking for something that resembled Jules' name. Prather wouldn't even have a phone if his agent didn't both insist upon it and make sure the bill was paid. Bills never held his attention long enough to warrant real, sustained effort. Along the same lines, remembering phone numbers was beyond Prather. He often made others record their numbers in his phone if they insisted upon him having their number, offering his ignorance of technology as an excuse. Most people bought it.

There. Jules Dayton. Prather pushed the button, let the

phone dial.

"Hel-lo?" a woman's slightly scratchy voice said. Prather pictured her hovering over the phone, trying to decide how many rings before she could pick up, how many before it said pretense or disinterest, how few before it said desperation? He could see her: wearing a tank top and pajama bottoms, both a size too small for her chubby frame, both in some insouciant color Prather would use only to paint a mocking picture of George Bush mated with Hello Kitty—if he ever bothered to paint such an overtly political piece. He had no idea if Jules was blind to the shape of her body or just hoped others were. Prather was not so body conscious—his own body was tight with muscle and he had never worked a minute for any of it—he did not need those he connected with to be anything other than willing and vibrant. He would draw the line when a person's weight became a hindrance so inescapable it called out to him as art—his eyes examining the curves and failing to see the individual any longer; the pocked flesh and rather grotesque arabesques of flabby rolls—as something other than what it truly was: a person. That was too much for Prather.

He preferred to let people's judgments of themselves determine their worth in his eyes. If you could see beauty in your muffin-top—or could effectively pretend, displaying it with such earnestness to the world—it could be attractive to Prather. It was self-hate, deep and slashing insecurity which turned Prather's lust into seething disdain.

Jules had been one of those he suspected of displaying her

body as pretense, as if to say that she knew she was fat and expected you to focus on the beautiful aspects—as she supposedly had, as she desperately wanted you to believe— when something in her manner, something in her style of dress echoed her true feelings: that she was in fact fat and unattractive. But it had not been overt, thus Prather had been able to let his mind wander along the path Jules had lain, finding her lush and womanly in all the right ways, her curves soft, pliable, compelling.

"Jules," Prather said, a decision made. Even as he said it, he sat down in front of his oft-forgotten computer and saw the heap of messages marked "From: Jules Dayton," though he could not remember having given her his email address—but that hardly mattered—his mononym made him easy to find on the internet. Quickly realizing she would want soothing for his lack of response to those emails—and likely to the multitude of calls she had placed as well—Prather called up an easy lie. "I misplaced my phone, Jules. I get lost painting sometimes," he said. "But I finally checked my email this afternoon and saw you sent... *a few*." That should suffice.

After a little pause Jules replied, "Yeah." Her voice sounded strained, like she was nervous. But Prather didn't have time to contemplate the why because Taty came rushing past the rows of hanging sheets separating Prather's space in the warehouse from the space she shared with her husband Vich and their kid, Anton. Seeing Taty made Prather suddenly remember he hadn't seen Anton in weeks—maybe months. Not that Prather cared. The less he saw of Anton the better—he was never

54

prepared to deal with the kid, even though he wasn't really a kid anymore—with the inevitable thorniness of their relationship.

He had lived with those three for over a decade, since Anton had been a mere toddler. Prather had watched Anton grow, had taught the boy about painting, taught him how Prather saw art, something Prather himself had never been shown externally—he had to arrive at it alone, first-generation. Anton had taken up Prather's words—his time and his energy—like a quietly dedicated, deviously methodical sponge. It had only been a mild shock when Prather had woken up after passing out from an extended painting spree to find pre-teen Anton—the kid couldn't have been more than eleven; hell, might have even been nine or ten when Prather had woken up to find the boy's mouth full of Prather's cock.

It wasn't shocking to find the kid was gay—that had been obvious to both Prather and Anton's parents—they had openly discussed the possibility only days after Prather had met them, despite Anton being a child. They believed in letting Anton be Anton, as unstructured by their interference as possible. Prather believed there was wisdom in that—had agreed with their approach—only suddenly finding issue with it when he had woken up near to cumming in the kid's mouth. Nothing in Prather's life had prepared him for *that* moment, for the hurt in the kid's eyes when Prather told him it was wrong, not because of their ages, not wholly, but because Anton *hadn't asked* and because Prather didn't feel *that* way about him. Anton had run away for the first time shortly after.

Seeing Taty brought all that back more clearly than it had in Prather's mind for a long, long time. Shit, the kid was definitely over eighteen by now—*maybe I should paint him.* There was something in Taty's expression—she was high, she always was—she was definitely troubled about something. Remembering he was still on the phone, Prather mumbled, "OK. Hold on for a second, OK?" He didn't even wait to hear a response, just held the phone loosely at his side, gave his full attention to the worried Taty.

"Prath, I've been looking for Anton for eighteen days now, he's never stayed away this long, have you heard from him?" Taty asked. Of course, Prather had told Taty and Vich what had happened with Anton way back when. He had been shocked—something he was not used to feeling—when they had both tried to give him their blessing. Saying if Anton was *ready* for sex, they were glad it was with someone as cool as Prather. Prather had spluttered at them, the effort of holding back accusations and recriminations warring inside him with specifically chosen desire not to ever discount another's way of living. He had asked them to talk to Anton: *ask him not to do it again.* Though Anton rarely did as his parents asked, he never touched Prather again without permission; that Prather knew, at least.

Prather shook his head in the negative at Taty and Vich, told them hadn't seen Anton and suggested maybe their son had found somewhere else to live. Or that he was at Trevie's.

Taty seemed somewhat mollified, but she still asked Prather to make some calls, see if he could locate her son. After all, sharing the same loft space with Prather and the other artists who lived there, Anton knew most everyone Prather did. He promised her he would make some calls and Taty clasped her frail, spindly arms around him—her flowing clothes stank of old sweat and the linseed oil she used in her furniture reworking. At times, Taty both looked and felt like a figure of sticks wrapped in oily rags, waiting to be lit on fire—and yet she was still vibrant (not in a way Prather found sexually attractive, though he had fucked her and Vich both many times,) still at one with her life force and art—a truth Prather adored about her. Vich was the same—to a lesser degree, to a more inconsistent degree—but he hardly ever left his art-space these days, convinced his life's work was always on the cusp of creation. Though, to Prather's knowledge, the man hadn't raised his hand to write in years. Taty released Prather and totted away, her clothes billowing around her while the sheets dividing the loft billowed around the clothes.

Prather suddenly felt the phone, heavy and hard in his hand, realized he still had Jules on the other line. Only vaguely remembered why he had called her in the first place. Thoughts of Anton kept invading his mind-space and he couldn't concentrate, but he knew he *needed* to see Jules again. Had to ascertain if something between them needed either exorcising or embracing.

Anton first.

"Listen, I have to go. But I was hoping to see you again. Are you free tonight?" Prather said, unsure what he would be doing later that night, unsure if he would bother to remember setting plans with Jules—only knowing that making plans with her would be more *likely* to spur him to follow through than not.

He heard the breathlessness of her reply, the excitement she tried, and failed, to hold back. "Um. Yeah, I was going to go see a movie with my Davis, but he's probably going to cancel anyway, so yeah, I'm free, what did you have in mind?" Prather didn't have anything in mind yet, and saw no reason to lie.

"I don't have anything in mind yet, and I don't have time to figure it out right now, I've got something important to handle. Have to help one of my housemates with something." Still unsure if he would bother showing up, Prather decided to be a bit more concrete than he would normally be. Something about Jules tugged hard at him. He knew it must be worked through—he couldn't risk letting the unknown color his painting, disengage him from his art. He had to embrace things which churned below his conscience—they could easily consume the vital part of him otherwise, could cause him to fail in his art. He shivered at the thought.

"How about we meet at Union Square, outside Virgin Records, say eleven?"

Prather chose the spot because he knew Anton liked to frequent sex shops nearby, would occasionally meet up with men in Union Square. He would go there and look for the kid and meet up with Jules after; unless he ended up blowing her off. Her voice was more controlled now; she was definitely making an effort, which made Prather smile. He liked people who could actualize self-control, and people who made an effort.

"Um, yeah," Jules said, her voice choking as soon as Prather had thought positively about her control. "Eleven is OK. I'll see you then."

Nodding, Prather responded, "Great. See you then, Jules." He ended the call and Jules was completely gone from his thoughts. Setting the phone down, he went to find some clothes. Prather dressed in a pair of paint-splotched khaki pants, some boat shoes, and an old t-shirt. Whom the t-shirt belonged to he had no idea, but it was emblazoned with lyrics from the eighties song, "The Warrior." It read "Shooting at the Walls of Heartache" surrounded by brightly colored stars, the word "bang!" written over each. Prather recognized the song —if not the shirt. He had once painted obsessively for hours while listening to the track on repeat, only stopping to smoke weed or mix paint. He had never understood why, and the painting had been god awful, and although the shirt reminded him of that fact, he didn't want to toss it.

Clothes shouldn't go in the garbage.

Dressed, Prather wandered out of his space, stopped to talk to some of the others as he passed. Most people living in the loft were transitory. Only Taty, Vich, Anton, Prather himself, and a woman named Loni could be considered permanent residents. All the people lounging on the ratted sofas and sitting cross-legged on carpet remnants were vaguely familiar.

Some had lived there for a good while, months or so. Yet he recalled very little about any of them. He absorbed their fawning over his work and the occasional flirtation with equanimity before waving himself on and out of the loft. Outside, it was the dim of late afternoon. The building's shadow heralded night without copying it. People moved on the streets, most dressed in business casual. The whole area had changed so drastically in the last decade. He was sure the loft he shared with the others was one of the last of its kind in Dumbo.

A sad thought.

As he walked, Prather made calls, starting with Trevie. He didn't expect Trevie to answer, had already determined he would need to physically visit the dealer's place to learn anything useful. Trevie was a strange bee on the phone. It was likely that Taty had asked for Prather's help for this very reason: she herself had been unable to reach Trevie on the phone, or had reached him and gotten nothing of use.

When Trevie didn't answer Prather's third call, he called other numbers, finding little success. The only person who answered, was definitely NOT the Malcolm Prather had called, claimed to have "no idea, bro." Sighing, Prather put the phone in his pocket and caught the 5 train for Trevie's apartment, still debating whether or not he would remain in Union Square long enough after searching for Anton to meet up with Jules.

Trevie lived in East Flatbush. Not a short—nor easy— subway ride from Dumbo. When Prather finally emerged from the steps at the Newkirk & Nostrand Ave., he found himself surrounded by other, darker brown faces. Many of them distinctly West African, others obviously Haitian. The neighborhood had a feeling about it, as though it were bipolar. Could become manic at any moment, with no warning shot fired.

Navigating the bustling street, Prather found himself outside a huge, blocky building. Twin to tens of others, all of them squatting, like family that wouldn't get a job, wouldn't get off the couch, and wouldn't leave. He buzzed Trevie. No answer. Prather had been through this before. Had been inside Trevie's apartment before while Trevie's mind refused to acknowledge the buzzer. Prather leaned on the button and refused to let up.

After several minutes, a resident came up and opened the door. Eyeing Prather with suspicion, the resident looked at his clothes and unkempt brown hair. Likely assumed Prather was one of the innumerable junkies who bought their fix from Trevie's apartment on the third floor. Prather's one and only experience in life which involved a gun pressed to his head had occurred in that very apartment. It had been a valuable lesson in not letting a drug dealer like Trevie talk you into doing favors. They never worked out as planned.

Standing outside Trevie's third floor apartment, Prather banged resolutely on the door, stopping only long enough to switch hands. Before long, the door slitted open. He didn't recognize the short, busty girl--freckle-faced, maybe twenty years old—wearing only a black bra and a pair of men's boxer shorts. Her eyes were drawn with thick eyeliner, a half-smoked cigarette dangling from her lips.

"Yeah?" she asked pointedly.

Prather blinked, gave his best smile. "Trevie around?"

She eyed him warily, looking him up and down several times. She never quite met his eyes, but snorted just enough to be heard without disturbing her cigarette. Little swirls of smoke came out of her nose, like a petulant dragon. She turned and shouted, her voice carrying over the thumping, ambient music. Typical Trevie stuff—ATB or something like it—played on a continuous loop through cheap wireless speakers installed into every room of the apartment.

"Oy! Trev! There's a gay dude here to see you!" the girl shouted. She looked back, appraising Prather, a question mark in her black-encircled, slightly downcast eyes. She cocked her hips to one side, tilted her head, and looked at Prather's chest, waiting. Prather kept smiling at her.

Her eyes narrowed. Maybe she wondered why Prather did not leer at her. She was tiny. Her waist uncovered by clothes, a round ass which tight boxers couldn't hide, and handful-sized breasts, perky with youth, pink areolas almost glowing half-exposed underneath her lacy bra. Had circumstances been different, Prather would have leapt at her. So to speak.

Maybe some other time.

Trevie wandered up from a bedroom, his jerky movements between a dance, a stumble, and a balancing act. When Trevie looked past the girl and saw Prather, his face lit up.

"Damn, Tuesday, move the hell out of the way! Let the hot

piece of ass in." Trevie snickered behind his own dangling cigarette. *Is the girl's name actually Tuesday? Perhaps Trevie can't remember her name and is just calling her that because it is, in fact, Tuesday.* She showed no sign either way, but did step immediately out of his way, sycophantically copying Trevie's pleasure at the sight of Prather. She waited near the door while Prather passed and carefully shut it behind him.

"Yo! Prath, my man! What brings you around?" Trevie asked, acting out his part, saying his lines as faithfully as ever. The man was erratic to the point of being useless most times, but in some things he was constant as nightfall. Prather turned his smile on Trevie, pleased to see the usual curl of the man's upper lip, showing he had not yet fried his brain to the point of not getting *it*. Prather loved that about Trevie. That he got *it*.

"I'm looking for Anton, Trevie. Have you seen him?" Prather said as the three of them sat down on the squarish, sectional sofa. It was covered in stitched-together sheets, one of them obviously emblazoned with the faces of some boys called N*SYNC. Trevie leaned forward and banked his cigarette in an ash tray, pulled out a water bong from the space under the coffee table, and filled it with crystal meth while he talked.

"Nah, ain't seen the little squirt in at least a month. Shocking, right? He's probably got a sugar daddy somewhere or something. Otherwise, you know, he'd be *around*." Trevie wrapped his lips delicately around the stem of the water bong, oblivious to the look of annoyance on the face of

Tuesday, who clearly coveted the first hit for herself. Prather decided she must be more than the usual company. Trevie puffed at the bong lightly—pulling the cut off, there wasn't much—taking a massive hit. His chest expanded mightily as he did so. Holding the bong away from himself, Trevie exhaled. Trevie exhaled a cloud of meth smoke, proudly turning his head halfway through to blow it on Tuesday. She sniggered, took a deep breath, inhaling some of it. Trevie dutifully passed the bong to her. *Yes, definitely more than the usual company.* Trevie always declared his rankings in such ways.

Tuesday hit the bong several times, burning the torch far too close to the bowl. Such an action would normally have sent Trevie into fits, but he was staring glassy-eyed at Prather. When Tuesday offered Prather the bong he waved it off.

"I don't have any idea where he's at, Prath-bro," Trevie said, the seriousness of his tone not at all in sync with the glazed look on his face. Trevie genuinely liked few people, Prather had learned. The dealer adored Taty and Anton. And apparently now whomever this Tuesday was. Trevie would think Prather coming around to look for Anton was beyond the pale. Enough to indicate something worthy of concern.

"Taty must be having a *fit*, if she sent *you* over here to look for Anton," Trevie said, accepting the bong from Tuesday. It was now completely emptied of meth. He set it on the coffee table. The torch lighter he placed on the silicone mat next to the ash tray. "But really, bro, the squirt is what, nineteen, twenty by now? It's not like he's still fourteen or some shit and out selling his mussy at fourgies and sex clubs anymore. She needs to let go, bro."

So, Anton is definitely over eighteen now. Guess I missed that.

Trevie knew Taty very well. As usual, his insight was dead on. Prather nodded. Out of the corner of his eyes, he saw Tuesday playing with her tits. Her bra was pulled down to reveal a bar piercing in each nipple, which she gently twisted, moaning and chewing on her bottom lip as did so. Prather got an erection.

"Taty says he's never dropped out for this long. It's been almost a month now. No word at all," Prather said, forcing himself not to focus on Tuesday, letting the words sink in on Trevie. Anton's meth habit demanded Trevie's good will. The kid rarely found enough money to purchase it elsewhere for the low "at cost" price Trevie always gave him. Sometimes, Prather knew, Trevie outright gifted it to the kid for nothing.

Prather wondered—knowing Trevie as he did—if the dealer had ever pimped Anton out. It certainly was possible, but equally as likely, if it had happened that it had been Anton's idea all along.

"Well. Like I said," Trevie said, reaching over to refill the water bong, "Probably found a rich, old sugar daddy with a hot connection."

That made sense also. Because otherwise Anton would have been spending said sugar daddy's money at Trevie's to ensure Anton kept sufficient meth supplies. "But *listen*, Prath-bro. I'll make some calls. See if I can put out the word we need to find his little bitch ass, K?"

Prather nodded, aware it was the best he was going to get from Trevie. Unless Anton showed up or called the dealer himself. Trevie filled the bong and started to smoke when he noticed what Tuesday was doing and smiled hungrily at her, his lips curving around the stem of the bong. Staring at the girl the whole time, Trevie took another massive hit but didn't let the smoke out. He brought his lips to hers and exhaled directly into her mouth. That was the closest thing to love Prather thought he would ever see from Trevie. Tuesday let out a whimper as she blew the huge cloud of smoke out. She leaned back on the sofa, leaving a hand on an exposed nipple, the other disappearing into her boxers. Prather knew it was time to leave. Or join in. *Decision time.* Weirdly, Jules tugged at him. More so than Anton's disappearance even. *How odd is that?* Feeling that tug, Prather knew he would not be able to enjoy sex with the tweaking girl. So he coughed to get Trevie's attention.

Trevie turned to look at him with a nasty leer and inclined his head and eyes at Tuesday. His expression said, "Can you believe it?" or maybe, "Jackpot!" It was hard to tell with Trevie. The dealer saw Prather's expression. Frowned, as if he knew Prather would like to try the girl but was purposefully refusing. Something clicked in Trevie's face. Trevie was assuming Prather was more interested in Anton than Tuesday. *He thinks I want Anton.* But Trevie shrugged. He knew Prather well. Sometimes Prather just didn't want sex.

"A'ight, Prath-bro. I'll make those calls. In a bit. You know, once *she's* had enough. Peace out, Prath." Trevie insisted on the idiotic multi-step handshake he always proffered when Prather left. As soon as their hands parted, Trevie was fully ignoring Prather for Tuesday, not bothering to wait before literally slapping the girl across her face as the door slammed shut and she moaned with excitement.

Prather sighed and went on his way.

Pauline

Hell's Kitchen, Manhattan, New York City.

"To attempt to force to action; urge; spur on."

"Would you like some more wine, Miss?" the waiter proffered, leaning down to ask. His feature set was bland as his face was smooth. Handsome and unlined.

Pauline resisted the temptation to pat her hair, to pull back any loose strands. It was not that she was attracted to the boy. After all, he was probably still a teenager. Well, probably not that young. But still younger than either of Pauline's two grown boys. She was not going to do *that*. Yet she increasingly found a hard desire within herself to assert that she could still be attractive to such men, to boys who had just left the word boy behind. Perhaps it had something to do with Jack and Mason both finally being married. Both soon to be fathers, and both finding their mother had given them the wrong idea about what a wife was willing to do. Poor Kahne. Jack's little doll of a wife had called Pauline crying just the week before because Jack had insisted that if Kahne were "half the woman Mom is... then I wouldn't have to tell you to take care of this shit! To make sure the clothes are done right and that dinner is ready! For fuck's sake Kahne! It's not like it takes a great deal of intelligence to do these things. You went to college for fuck's sake! *Get a clue!*"

Of course, Kahne had repeated this to Pauline, watching intently when Pauline winced near the end. The two were friends. At least, Pauline considered the girl her friend. She was not sure Kahne felt the same. Pauline suspected the girl mostly wanted to please Jack and hoped being close to Pauline would finally do the trick. Pauline knew that would never work. It hadn't worked with Jack and Mason's father. She didn't think it would work with his sons either. But how to share that particular truth with Kahne had not yet occurred to Pauline.

As she thought of Jack and Mason, Pauline sighed sadly. *Where did I go wrong with those boys?* They seemed more like men who had grown up in Pauline's generation than their own. They were unapologetic in their chauvinism, had both chosen wives who reinforced that behavior. Nothing Pauline had said made much of a difference. The boys listened to her about some things—when she could corner them, anyway—but they didn't change. Maybe it was too late. Maybe she had failed, needed to accept it. Quitting wasn't her way, though. The idea of having grandchildren raised in such a manner mortified her. Still, there was nothing she could think to do about it. Except offer herself as an escape route whenever possible. A niggling thought troubled her: *if my boys turned out so selfish, it must be my fault. For the man-less upbringing I gave them. For not being good enough to keep a husband.* Maybe, just maybe, Jack and Mason's kids would be better than Jack and Mason. Despite having assholes for present fathers—as opposed to assholes for absentee fathers.

"I raised a pair of assholes," Pauline murmured to herself.

She giggled into her wine. Thinking of her boys as assholes —because it was true, though she had never said it aloud before—made her feel strange and amused. *Lord help me, it's true.*

She told the waiter, "No, thanks." Her anxiety immediately lessened once the handsome boy wandered off to another table. Pauline looked down at her watch, sighed heavily, smoothed her hair again. *He* was late. Almost a half-hour now. She had been waiting, lost in her thoughts. No call. Nothing.

This is what is wrong with meeting men on the Internet.

Just as she thought the whole date experiment was a flat out bad idea, the door across the restaurant opened. A tall, broad shouldered woman—with a mustache—walked in. The whole place was full of odd people, outlandish outfits. Drag queens, drag kings, lavishly dressed women, equally loudly dressed men. Pauline had chosen the place partly because it was down the street from her Hell's Kitchen apartment, three blocks from 60th St., but also because she knew the crowd would not bat an eyelash at the sight of her and Ray having dinner together. *On a date.* A rush suffused her at that thought. It had been a long time since she went on a date. Of any kind.

Ray spotted her, offered a huge smile under his prodigious mustache. He sauntered over, his gait uneven, still getting used to walking heels. Even the clunky strap-on affairs Pauline could see he wore.

God those are awful.

Pauline looked him over. He *was* nicely built for a man his

70

age. The mustache gave him distinction, but his taste in women's clothes was atrocious. Pauline had worn something alike to Ray's outfit. Back when Jack and Mason had been *toddlers* in the early 1980's. A sudden surge of doubt coursed through her.

I'm not ready for this. I'm not ready to be dating a man whom I need to give women's fashion advice to.

But a persnickety voice countered: You're *not going to find anyone else, Pauline. You're fat. Old. Ugly. Broken.*

None of which she could dispute. She had gotten to the point where her doctor had used the words "morbidly obese." Far more humiliating, Mason had refused to invite her to Jaqueline's baby shower, saying the former beauty queen would be *"too embarrassed"* to introduce Pauline to her friends.

It's not nice!

She imagined for a moment that perhaps Jaqueline *deserved* the asshole card she had been dealt in marrying Mason. Pauline's indignation intensified.

How DARE that tactless little bitch say such a thing? Pauline *was* fat. And old. And ugly. She would not dispute those facts. Yet she was also wildly successful. Had sent *two* sons to Harvard, tuition fully paid. She owned an entirely too-large apartment in Manhattan *and* a manor house in Connecticut. Her last book had sold over half a million copies. Had been featured on Oprah's Book Club. And *that* strumpet was *embarassed* by *her*? Pauline sniffed in derision just as Ray reached the table.

Oh God I hope he doesn't think that was for him.
Get it TOGETHER Pauline!

Pauline stood up. Ray reached for her hand, kissed the back of it. Pauline giggled, surprised by the ridiculousness of the gesture as much as she was charmed by the silly, unexpected romance of it. Men just didn't do that anymore.

"Pauline! You look incredible! *Beautiful!* I'm so sorry I'm late. I sincerely hope you can forgive me," Ray said. His voice sounded exactly as it had over the phone. The deep timbre soothing. Full of assurance. At decided odds with everything else about him visually, save the mustache. She had known about the mustache, but she hadn't seen a photo. Ray hadn't wanted to send her a picture, instead assiduously telling her he would rather not have her form an opinion of him in *that* way, and that he hadn't wanted to see one of her, either. She had been oddly impressed by that. *Did he just say I'm beautiful?*

Pauline blushed. Her hands rose to smooth her hair again before she commanded them to stop. She had no idea how to respond to Ray's kind words. *Do I tell him he looks handsome? Dashing? Or is pretty appropriate? Even if it isn't true?* Ray saw the confusion spelled out on her face, but he held Pauline's hand across the table, gestured with his eyes for both of them to sit. Ray smiled graciously at her.

"It's OK. Pauline, use whatever words you need to use, I won't be offended."

It's like he heard my thoughts!

She took a deep breath, annoyed she had been holding it in

the first place. "Well, you look dashing, Ray," she said, her voice steadier than she felt. He winked at her, ruffling his mustache. "And don't worry about the lateness," Pauline continued, "I'm sure you had a good reason." She was not sure of that at all, but it was polite to say so.

And it doesn't matter. Does he really think I'm beautiful? How is that possible?

"Not really, I have to say. I had trouble getting dressed and then I ran into a friend of my son's and had to stop the cab to catch him, then after talking to him I had to catch another cab. Not a good reason at all. *You* deserve better, but I promise to try harder next time."

Pauline stared at him incredulously.

He's so honest!

She put her hand to her chest, her heart thumped hard. *Maybe, just maybe he had meant it when he called her beautiful.* His eyes certainly were drinking her in, and she could not remember the last time *that* had happened. Perhaps Jack and Mason's father once looked at her that way, before he ran off. Pauline pushed thoughts of the man away before his name surfaced.

"Well, shall we order? I didn't know your son lived in New York. I assumed your family was still in Louisiana," Pauline said, still somehow managing to keep her voice steady and her hands away from her hair.

Ray chuckled. "Honestly, Pauline, I don't know where my son lives anymore. It's one of the reasons I had to talk to his friend. I had hoped... but well. Let's not go into that right now,

OK? I want to hear more about *you*. You have two boys, don't you?" Ray said, looking over his menu at her.

Pauline bit back the questions she wanted to ask about Ray's son. There was a *story* there—and she thrived on stories. But he seemed to like her. She didn't want to worry about that just yet. He seemed as genuinely good a man in person as he had come across online and over the phone. She would have to trust he would open up after they knew each other better. Pauline had learned a sharp lesson about closed off men. They were emotionally stunted. And she was far too old for that.

Might as well chase after the waiter. It would be just as pointless.

Ray seemed blessedly *not* that way.

"Jack and Mason. They're twins. 27 and both just married in the last year. Both expecting children in the next month." Her voice stayed steady but even as she mentioned her soon-to-be grandchildren, the expected, *required* happiness surge did not come.

What is wrong with me?

Ray was giving her his full attention now, the menu set aside. Pauline raised hands to her hair and brushed it back, only realizing in mid-action she had done so at all. She blushed. Ray beamed at her, undeterred. She wanted to deflect. To ask him about his kids. But she remembered his admonition and bit the question back.

He doesn't want to talk about that right now.

"Jack and Mason, nice solid names. Do they know if they're having boys or girls?" Ray asked.

"Both of them are having boys," Pauline said. "I think Jack has decided on Dallas for the name and Mason on Rush." Pauline grimaced a little at the second name.

Ray noticed.

"As in Rush Limbaugh?" Ray posited with a slight grin. Pauline nodded and blushed. "Mason is a... Republican. He seems to believe quite strongly that the answers to every social and fiscal problem can be solved, *simply*, by cutting government spending and letting the 'free' market run unfettered. I've *tried* to talk him out of it. God *knows* I have. But he just brushes me off." Pauline gave a little laugh, as if those brush-offs were nothing. Even though they stabbed her liver every time they drifted through her thoughts. Ray reached over the table and grabbed her hand, squeezed it.

"Pauline, we *can't* be responsible for our kids' thoughts anymore. I mean, *you* can't." Ray smiled wide, his teeth were a little crooked and Pauline found it charming. "Our children are who they are. All we can do is love them and hope they will love others in return. I only wish I'd come to that knowledge a long time ago. Perhaps my kids would actually like me now." Pauline snickered inside, but withheld the expression from her features. That was the kind of lovey-dovey crap she used in her novels. To hear it from a man's mouth, was, well... it was funny.

And quite possibly also true.

"You're right of course. I just worry, you know? That maybe I failed him somehow. That maybe I could fix it all, somehow. I just want him to be *happy*. But he seems destined to grow old, hating everyone who isn't as talented, or educated, or wealthy as himself." She breathed deeply. There! She had said it. Had said something *bad* about one of her children. Out loud to another soul, to a relative stranger. It was liberating. Ray smiled and nodded, all apparent understanding.

"Would you like to order?" Ray asked, tone light

Pauline nodded, "Sure." Sensing the couple were now ready, the handsome young waiter sauntered over.

"You all ready?" the delicate man said, pulling out a pad and pencil. Studying him, it suddenly occurred to Pauline that he was not a man at all. Rather, he was a very thin, very boyish *girl*. She beamed at the waiter/waitress, pleased to have seen such, to have figured it out. The waitress beamed back, her face showing she was a little confused by Pauline's wide smile.

I wonder what she would want me to call her? Him? Waiter? Waitress?

Ray filled the space. "Yes, we are." He waved Pauline to go first. She ordered the honey-dipped fried chicken, carefully watching Ray to see if he reacted. He smiled appreciatively. "*That* sounds excellent," Ray said, "I'll have the same." Pauline shifted in her seat, unsure if she was nervous or excited or what. The waitress had not batted an eyelash at Ray's cross-dressing, Pauline's weight, or the fact they were holding hands across the table.

A sudden, terrible notion washed over Pauline.

Had the waitress assumed I'm a man in women's clothes as

76

well?

The idea was so horrifying that try as she might to push it away, it wouldn't budge. She blurted the words before she could clamp them inside.

"I'm *not* a man, you know," Pauline said to the waitress, clapping her hand over her mouth immediately after. The waif waitress shuttered her eyes in confusion or disdain, it was hard for Pauline to tell, and nodded as she re-opened them.

"I hadn't thought you were, *ma'am?*" the waitress said, a half-question obvious in her tone. "I asked if that was all you wanted?"

Pauline's face blazed and she looked away, focusing on the accoutrements of the table, not wanting to make eye contact with either Ray or the waitress.

"Yes. I think that will be all, for now," Ray said.

What does he mean by all?

Is the date over?

Pauline pulled in forced, labored breaths. *Christ, but dates are so much easier to write in novels than to actually endure.*

Why am I so bad at this?

Bad at raising my boys. Bad at keeping myself healthy. Bad at dating. Bad at recognizing a waitress as a girl.

And let's be honest, my novels are pseudo-Southern Gothic vampire trash!

"Pauline," Ray said, his voice calm and compelling. It pulled Pauline's eyes to his with a magnetic jerk. His eyes were a puddled blue. They likely could be hard but were so readily kind. Ray reached over and held out his hands, gestured for hers. "It's OK. Really. It's *new* to me too. Believe it or not. I've spent most of my life hiding who I really am. Dressing like a man. Like I thought a man *should*. It's only in the past year that I've allowed myself to explore who I really am. The Ray I'm *meant* to be. I don't expect it to be easy. And I don't expect everyone, myself included, to get it right the first time. Or the second or fifth. Or tenth. It's a process, like becoming a vampire. Like The Jesuit in *The Honeysuckler's Kiss*. Heard of it?" His tone and words were as kind as the blue of his eyes implied. Pauline was flabbergasted, wondering where this man had been all her life. Angry at herself for embracing the cliché, even in thought. So angry she missed exactly what he had said at the end of the little speech.

He's read one of my novels? One of my older ones, no less!

Where was he was when I was thirty and alone? With two angry boys? And only a paycheck away from living in my car... with only the vaguest idea of The Honeysuckler's Kiss *in my mind? When the only dates I could find were those I put to paper and invented? When I still had a waist-line?*

Pauline grasped at composure. "Um. Thank... you, Ray." She let him squeeze her hands. Let herself *feel* the rush which came with the squeeze. "I don't think I've *ever* known anyone like you."

Ray beamed. "Truthfully, I'm not sure I know myself. This is *all* so new. But I was never a very good father or husband the first time around. I'm *determined* to be a better person this time. It's kind of funny. Putting on a skirt... it freed me from all that baggage. Let me be the man I should have always been. Reborn, as cheesy as that sounds. Only I got to keep the wisdom I've picked up along the way." He laughed. "What little I've managed to retain that is. My son used to tell people I've only ever said five wise things." Another laugh, this one forced. "I kept the wisdom, but let go of the spite, the fear and the hatred, Pauline. And I have to say, it feels *great*. Like being here with you tonight feels."

She gaped. It all sounded so great.

Too good to be true. It must be.

Gently, she squeezed his hand back for the first time. Allowing herself more of the moment, Pauline shoved her doubts aside: *this might be the real thing!* She barely suppressed a shiver of excitement. She hoped he would invite her back to his place, or invite himself back to hers. The idea of being in his arms tonight was the electricity turning her dynamo. She did not think she could be the one to do it, but she would not say no if he were to ask.

"That's amazing Ray, really. I doubt you could have been as bad a father as you claim. Or husband." And she didn't believe he could have. *No one can change that radically, can they?* Such change took more than most people realized. Something Pauline had learned writing novels: you can't go from A to Z without touching the letters between.

Ray sighed wistfully.

"Cathy, that's my ex-wife..." He gave Pauline a beseeching look, examining her to see if she was OK with talking about his ex. She squeezed his hand again. "I was not very good to her, Pauline. I suppose I loved her in the beginning. And she gave me two beautiful children. But I think now maybe I just loved her for having those kids. I can't say I ever *liked* her much. I was cruel to her so many times. Made her suffer for my failed choices, because she was emblematic of the me I knew was hidden inside, desperate to come out. I'll never live that cruelty down. Not sure I ever want to. It was horrid of me, to stay with her for so long. Belittling her, berating her, blaming her. Because I made that mistake, you know?"

And Pauline did know. She had written men much like Ray's description of himself in her novels. Had often enjoyed killing them off in especially creative ways, leaving their widows free to marry handsome Italian nobility or Greek shipping magnates or former English RAF pilots. But she had never written one of those men capable of such self-awareness, such honest ability to look at himself and take the blame. She hadn't known men could be that way. It wouldn't have felt real or honest for Pauline to write such a man; even her most amazing hero wasn't that way. He hadn't needed to be: he was perfect and would never do those things in the first place, and thus never need to understand himself enough to admit his own failings. Only now did she see the flaw in her creation, see that such a man was not perfect, but only appeared to be on paper. Her mind whirled and her body flushed with excitement and pleasure.

"I still hope for the best for her. But she didn't handle this well." Ray waved over his clothes and wig. "I tried to explain it to her. For some reason I tried to hold the marriage together despite the changes I was determined to undertake. Twenty-two years is a long time and even without love or like you *can* grow very used to person, you know?" Pauline nodded, though she was sure she didn't know. She had never had the chance to grow close to any man other than her sons. Their father had left her within weeks of getting her pregnant.

"But I eventually realized that was wrong of me as well. I couldn't, *shouldn't* expect Cathy to endure this change with me. Not when I had treated her so poorly, for so long. Not when she was against the change. It has worked out for the best, I think. And in the long run even Cathy'll be happier for it. I have to believe that. Our kids still haven't forgiven me and I suspect Cathy never will, but I still hope for it, as silly as that sounds."

But it isn't silly at all.

"Your kids will come around, Ray, just don't give up on them."

Like I want to give up on mine.

In an unrelated thought she wondered: *How pretty and thin is Cathy?*

"I hope so, Pauline, but I won't wait around for that. They have their own lives and I won't intrude on them. I was so distant and miserable to them as kids and teenagers. I tried— half-assed most of the time—to be there for them, but I know I never was. They are just beginning to deal with their resentment of me, I think. You would think the cross-dressing thing would be the big issue, but it wasn't." He smiled. Pauline was entranced. *You can't make this stuff up.*

"My son, Alex, he's gay, Pauline. Came out when he was

twelve if you believe that. I was horrible to him! Of course, I knew the truth about myself, about the real me, deep inside." Pauline wondered if he meant his bisexuality or the cross-dressing, both of which he had openly told her the first time they had chatted online. "I think I rode him so hard in the hope I could ride those things out of myself. Foolish, I know. When I finally told Alex about me, he rightfully called me a hypocrite and an asshole. Told me that he..." Ray laughed, "didn't care what kind of clothes I wore, it wouldn't change the waste of a person underneath." Ray shook his head and looked away. Pauline wiped a slight moisture away from her eyes. "Hearing that, well, Pauline, it made me think. And I started to work on changing myself for the better that day."

"Someday he'll give you the chance to show him that change, Ray, I promise," Pauline offered. Ray beamed.

"Very sweet of you to say, Pauline, but I'm not holding my breath. He's got to live his life on his own terms. I believe the saying is '*que sera, sera*' right?"

Pauline nodded eagerly. They stared at one another for a silent, hot moment. The whole restaurant slipped away from Pauline. When she returned to the moment, she felt she should tell him about Jack and Mason, about the secret fear she had failed in raising them. Of all men, surely he would understand, would commiserate!

The food arrived.

Pauline and Ray both leaned back away from each other as the waitress laid out their entrées and refilled their wine glasses. The pigeon-chested girl didn't say anything until everything was arrayed; she looked towards Ray, not Pauline, and said, "Can I get you anything else?"

Ray sighed. "No. Pauline?"

Pauline shook her head. "No, thank you." She let out a deep breath when the server departed. Ray's smile twitched his mustache. "Looks good."

She watched him eat with gusto that showed he was enjoying the food and the company. They talked between bites: about sex, politics, religion, and eventually, Pauline's books. She hadn't mentioned her pen name online, only told him that she was a writer. Hadn't even told him what kind of books she wrote, and yet he admitted he had read her first book. When she told him her pen name, he set his fork down and gave her a very serious, very frank and appraising look.

"You're Cathy's favorite writer. I've read several of your books. I mentioned one earlier!" Ray said as he grinned, huge and wide at her. "My son loved your books as well. I tried others besides *The Honeysuckler's Kiss*, but..."

Pauline laughed. It did bother her he was about to say he didn't like her work, a little at least, but she hadn't written her books for men like Ray. At least not the man Ray had been. A much larger part of her was warmed by his rejection of her other books. It meant he had the essence of a man underneath the tacky women's clothing. She blanched inside at that thought. *Is it OK to think that? Am I wrong to feel the need for Ray to be a man no matter what his appearance?* Pauline's mind raced until she zoned out.

"Pauline?" Ray asked, concerned.

"Yes? Oh, what? I'm so sorry, Ray. I got lost for a second," Pauline said. She was shocked, but not embarrassed. He had truly made her that comfortable. Like a bell going off, a need arose with her. Earlier she had wanted him to do the asking; to somehow insist they spend the night with one another. But now with this *need* coursing through her, she knew she would do the asking if he did not. She would urge and beg if she must. The desire, the ache to be wrapped in this man's arms was painful. It had been so long since she had felt anything like it; it was as though she hadn't truly been a woman at all for the past twenty-seven years, only a mother. It was as if, like Ray, she had been dressing for a part she had not believed in—only now seeing the folly of it all. The *wrongness*. Pauline's face flushed.

Ray smiled wide again, making the warmth of the flush on her face even stronger.

* * *

They were both having coffee when Ray set his cup down and looked at her. *Can he see the hunger on my face?* She brought her hands up, smoothing her hair back.

"Pauline, this might be..." Ray started, but Pauline interjected before he could get another word out.

"Yes!"

Ray laughed. A low, pulsing sound—unlike any other laugh Ray had made the entire dinner. "Let's catch a cab to my place," Ray said, half-chortling. Pauline might have disliked that in another man. In Ray she found it charming. He paid the restaurant bill, thanked the waitress, and they caught a cab down the street. The cabbie gave them strange looks through the rear-view mirror, but Pauline didn't mind. She snuggled into Ray, his right arm draped tightly over her, his warmth comforting her.

The ride wasn't long. Soon they were back at Ray's apartment. The tall man gently kissed Pauline, his mustache pleasantly tickling her face, the hairs surprisingly soft. Pauline didn't know how to feel: she was woozy, scared, and nervous. Hot with the need to be touched. They were kissing on the sofa in Ray's living room when the man pulled back.

"I'm going to go take all this stuff off, if that's OK?" Ray said. Pauline nodded, somewhat breathless. Wondering if he was going to undress in front of her. But he didn't. He wandered down a hallway and was gone.

Pauline looked around, her eyes almost immediately landing on a row of framed pictures sitting on a narrow table flush against a wall behind the sofa. Taking a hasty, nervous look around to be sure Ray wasn't returning, Pauline got up and went to look at those pictures. One was obviously a family portrait. There was Ray, mustache still emblazoned across his face, his hair short but full and his face tanned. *Is it my imagination or does his smile look forced*? Next to him was a frumpy looking woman, her hair styled in the manner of frumpy looking women. Pauline would have written it as "the last haircut given by a hairdresser who died of Parkinson's disease... in 1982." She laughed at her own thought.

Still, there was something about the woman in the photo. Surely this was Cathy. Something in her bright green eyes was compelling, leaving Pauline to wonder: *what did she look like when Ray fell for her?* This picture was not that old. The kids in it were nearly adults, or as close to it as to make no matter. Underneath Ray, his hand clasped on her shoulder, was a beautiful young woman. Her eyes as blue as her father's, but her features more balanced: her teeth straight and her hair a long, lustrous blond. The girl had a haughtiness in her expression which Pauline recognized it, or thought she did. *This girl doesn't like her family much. Feels herself above them. Though she tolerates her father's hand on her shoulder.* Pauline knew from the dinner conversation that Evelyn had been closer to Ray than Cathy. Also, that Ray had favored his kids over his wife. His daughter in particular. Which caused an unfortunate war between mother and daughter for Ray's attentions. Looking at that photo, Pauline sensed the truth of Ray's preference for his children. She looked at the young man next to Evelyn. *Unmistakably Alex.*

He wasn't smiling. While there was little resemblance between Evelyn and her parents, save for her father's eyes, Alex was a perfect mixture of both Ray and Cathy. So clearly their son, his eyes were as blue as his sister's. His hair was brown, though. Chestnut colored. And his nose was over-bold like his mother's, his chin prominent and slightly dented like his father's. But what struck Pauline most was that he somehow managed to look *alone* in the picture. As though he had his portrait taken in a studio two thousand miles away and then spliced in alongside the others. Beyond all that, there was a delicate nature to him. *Or do I see that because I know something of him from Ray?* There was no way to be sure.

Footsteps coming back down the hallway announced Ray's return. His wig was gone. So were the skirt and blouse and heels. He wore a set of sateen pajamas in a pastel green. Another set of the same were across his arm, presumably for her.

"If you want, there's a bathroom down the hall where you can change and get more comfortable. But if it's OK, I'd hoped you'd let me..." Ray said. His eyes gleamed with excitement as they trailed over her form. Pauline was pleased to hear nerves in his voice for the first time. The man was *finally* nervous!

Thank heavens!

"I..." Pauline started, unsure what to say as her face flushed again. Her skin felt unnaturally warm. *Christ, it isn't like I have never been with a man!* It just had been so long since anyone had looked at her that way, she was confused. Vulnerable.

"It's OK, Pauline. Really. I just want you to be happy. To feel good. We'll go your speed," Ray said.

Does this man ever say anything wrong?

Pauline smiled at him.

"I'm ready."

2Day

Midwood/East Flatbush, Brooklyn, New York City.

"To seek to influence by insistent arguments."

"Step. Ball Change. Step. Ball change!" 2Day murmured as she walked down Nostrand Ave. with Clarkless and Amber. For a Wednesday morning in December, it was unusually warm. Still cold enough she wore a scarf and heavy coat over her short skirt, black leggings, and black sweatshirt. "Step. Ball Change. Step. Step. Turn," she murmured again, acting out her words as she did so.

"I hate this fucking dancing shit!" 2Day bemoaned. "I didn't sign up for acting school to fucking learn how to perform dancing monkey tricks. I should have done what I wanted in the first place and studied Ancient Religions. At least then I could fucking feel smart. I feel like an organ grinder should be following me." 2day laughed. Amber and Clarkless laughed also, a half-second late. Only Clarkless sounded genuine to 2Day. 2Day eyed them from several steps ahead.

"So what's the plan?" Amber said after she stopped her weird laugh.

2Day shrugged, unsure what the plan was or should be. Clarkless usually made the plans when the three of them hung out. The first leg was always "get meth and get high."

But they had achieved that already... in spectacular fashion. *Thank fucking Mary for Trevie!* 2Day had not expected Trevie to be so gracious. Especially since he hardly knew Clarkless and had never met Amber. 2Day hadn't counted on Trevie's rampant lust. She had to admit—if only to herself—she had enjoyed watching Clarkless lick Trevie's asshole. Literally. In return for an eight-ball. Almost as much as she had enjoyed watching Amber deep-throat Trevie at the same time. If she had a dick it would have shot everywhere. But 2Day remained a woman, not that that was a bad thing, of course. The whole scene hadn't seemed exploitative to 2Day, as Clarkless had whined several times how much he wanted Trevie. And who wouldn't? The guy was all muscle and bones. Sleek and handsome in a feral way. Not to mention the fact he would fuck *anything* which would let him. There was something hot about that.

2Day suddenly realized Clarkless was too high right then to plan much beyond the little group's four block journey to the Newkirk #2 subway station. 2Day knew the route. Had traveled it alone the day before when she came to Trevie's in the first place. She was higher than Amber and Clarkless multiplied against each other now. *How long have I been awake now? Six days? Maybe eight? How many classes have I missed?*

2Day had forgotten about school until Amber and Clarkless had shown up at Trevie's looking for her. Now that she remembered class, she couldn't get it out of her head. The upcoming performance, the necessity that she do well or lose her scholarship. And thereby lose NYC.

"Step. Ball Change. Step. Step. Turn," 2Day murmured again, trying to perfect the part she hated most. She smiled, feeling through the meth haze she was finally getting traction on the moves. Now that she was applying herself.

"We're here, dears!" Amber's shrill voice exclaimed. And they were. The steep, descending stairs into the subway station seemed yet another dance 2Day had to master. One she was eminently more afraid she would fail at learning. Clarkless looked at her and laughed, wrapped his arm around her and guided them both down the stairs behind Amber. Who was hopping down the steps two at a time, barely catching herself each time she landed, chuckling with glee. When they reached the bottom of the stairs, Clarkless stopped and leaned over, out of breath. He was rail-thin with long hair wrapped up in a messy bun, strands of baby pink and yellow laced through the bun. His pointed face was angular and masculine, but at the same time pocked with occasional acne scars. Scars from picking. And his nose was a spotted constellation of very small blackheads. But 2Day only noticed those things when his face was close to hers. Otherwise the first things she always noticed were a pair of eyes so purple they had to be fake. But Clarkless never wore contacts, and 2Day would have known. The other thing was his nose, beak-like and curved, as though it had been broken. But again Clarkless claimed it hadn't. He even had a little story about it, how when he was still in the womb—according to some doctor, the specifics of the story were as thin as all of Clarkless's tales—an air bubble had somehow gotten between the cartilage forming in his nose, resulting in the odd curvature.

Whatever, it isn't important.

2Day supposed part of what she loved about Clarkless was those stories. Some of which had to be at least partly based in truth. But really, what was better than an entertaining friend? It's not like his stories were so outrageous she couldn't or didn't believe. They were like real stories, only inflated with supplementary decoration. And who didn't do that? Clarkless just did it better than anyone else 2Day had ever known. He was also brilliant. Could fix anything electronic. Even when he was so high he would shit on himself in the middle of the fixing. 2Day chuckled remembering that night. She still had that laptop. And it worked.

"What?" Clarkless demanded, laughing with her, recovered from his effort at helping her down the stairs. She eyed him meanly, a shared affection. Amber sidled back up to them, bouncing.

"I was just thinking about how much I like you, honey-bear," 2Day said, squeezing his hollowed cheeks.

He tweaked her nipples over her shirt. "Feeling's mutual pooter-bear." Amber frowned, feeling left out by the ritual. Which was understandable, because she was. Always would be. 2Day had only met Amber a few months before. They both attended New York Film Academy, were dorm-mates. A mutual love of *Buffy the Vampire Slayer* had led to discovery of a mutual love of crystal meth. The rest was rather unimportant. Amber was frumpy in every way 2Day was not.

Though Amber made up for some of it with a bounciness, a social effervescence 2Day could only match on her best days. Her abrasiveness was far too dominant. Larger girls and bounciness were not always the best pairing, but Amber made it work. Her curly red hair was cut short, hovering just above her ears for some reason, even though it made her look like a clown. Not a jokey clown, but a real, circus-y clown. Amber's super pale complexion and the nearly white powder-cake foundation she often wore didn't help the impression. Her large pendulous breasts and rotund belly underscored the effect. Still there was something *precious* about Amber. *If you can handle the annoyance of being her friend.* The situation was temporary, though. 2Day had discussed exactly that fact with Clarkless. They both knew Amber would grow out of all *this*. *What was the point of investing in someone who will outgrow you?*

There was no fear in 2Day of *that* with Clarkless. They had invested in each other. WERE invested in each other. They had done so long before either of them left Lafayette, Louisiana for New York City. Clarkless had left first, gracelessly leaving 2Day behind. Still, she had forgiven him for that. They had been very different people, even had different names, though their core friendship had been the same. Clarkless had always wanted to go to school in New York. When he got a full-ride at Parsons, 2Day had immediately realized the futility of trying to argue him out of it. Instead she had developed a plan of her own to follow—she had no dream of her own—why not settle for his? It was better than the alternative: working at *Mother Earth's* as a fucking sales girl selling pseudo-hippie kitsch to only vaguely interested aging baby-boomers and potheads.

Where was the future in that?

Besides, without Clarkless, 2Day didn't have any real friends left in Lafayette. They had all left long before. To California. To communes outside Portland. To Austin. To restless existences as couch-surfing party-monsters hopping from rave to rave. Or to dairy farms in Connecticut to reconnect with the banality of rural life. And prison. Lots went to prison. Including the only other person she and Clarkless had been close to: Lauren Gilbeaux.

What a bitch that girl was.

Still. I miss her.

2Day did hope Lauren was happy. She made a mental note to message her former friend on Facebook later in the hopes she would see it when she was released. 2Day looked at Amber and smiled. She saw Lauren there. Only fat... and talented. Amber did have a different life ahead of her. She would end up back in whatever bumfuck town in Kentucky she was from. Her glorious time in New York City would serve as the imaginary yardstick by which she measured— and found lacking—the rest of her future inanity in life. Those had been Clarkless's words. But that didn't make them any less true. 2Day looked at Clarkless as they passed through the turnstiles, each of them using Clarkless's MetroCard in turn. If his mother knew he was using the money she sent him to cosset 2Day in something—even something as base as a subway ride—the woman would be livid. She positively *hated*

93

2Day. The fact 2Day felt the same way about her was immaterial. She had, a few times, argued with Mrs. Rhondes, trying again and again and again to get the woman to like her. But it had been like running headlong into a wall of feathers. Or trying to cup fog. Clarkless's words, again.

Besides, the crotchety bitch had blamed 2Day for everything Clarkless did wrong. From the drugs to the arrests, to dropping out of LSU, to being a stone-cold, ass-eating faggot. Some of it *was* 2Day's influence. But Clarkless had been fucking guys long before he and 2Day became close. Was it her fault Mrs. Rhondes had walked in on Clarkless face-first into a grown man's hairy ass the very night after she had first been introduced to 2Day with the description "my favorite-est person ever!"? She had still been Karen then. And he'd simply been Clark then.

Mrs. Rhondes had stuck by her only child. Her golden boy son. Because she herself had no one else. Clarkless had told 2Day about some of the shit that woman put him through. When she was drunk and manic. Making him promise over and over again not to leave her in a nursing home when she was old, to always "be there for her." 2Day knew Clarkless would do it, too. If not in the way Mrs. Rhondes imagined. 2Day laughed at the image: of Mrs. Rhondes at eighty or ninety years old living with Clarkless in an apartment in San Francisco or New York City. Watching her early morning talk shows from a leather La-Z-Boy as Clarkless ambled home, stumbling and high; caked in dirt and sweat, some it his, most of it other men's—still high from the night before spent at a gay bathhouse or orgy.

What WILL the old bat say?

"You're laughing again," Clarkless said as they idled between two squarish columns, both covered in dirty white tiles, listening for an oncoming train. Amber was twirling around in a useless circle two columns down the platform. The station was empty for the most part. A few dark kids were talking animatedly as they occupied the sole wooden bench in the area. A lone old woman—she could have been Puerto Rican or Portuguese—clutched a Filene's Basement bag to her chest. She studiously paid no attention to anything but the tunnel in the direction the train should emerge from.

"I was picturing..." and 2Day told Clarkless exactly what she had been imagining, knowing he would find it funny. He did.

"Clark, honey, didya 'member to pick up tha' milk?" Clarkless said in a dead-on impersonation of his mother, Southern accent and all. He made his voice deeper, deeper than his voice ever was, to impersonate himself. "Um, no Ma, I *swallowed* it all!"

2Day shrieked with laughter. This brought Amber out of her circles and back into theirs. "What's so funny?" she said. When Clarkless tried to explain it to her, Amber just blinked, gave a false chuckle, and went back to spinning slowly in purposeless, precise circles.

"Make me a promise, Clarkless?" 2Day said, facing Clarkless and giving him her take me serious face. "A serious promise. No fingers crossed."

Clarkless stared, an extended expression, eyebrow arched. It did not mean anything, he was simply trying to push through his high, get to a sober moment. Because 2Day asked for it. Finally, he blinked rapidly and *there* he was.

"Sure thing. Miss Titties," Clarkless said. She hated that name and he knew it. Which was why he used it every time she asked him to be serious. It had long since ceased to really bother her. From Clarkless at least. She would shank anyone else who called her Miss Titties. Some random guy had given her that name after a night of post-rave fucking when they had gone to the store for orange juice and fruit to make them roll harder. The idiotic raver danced that liquid shit around her, only stopping in order to scream out a call to her as Miss Titties. Clarkless had laughed for days at that story. Had insisted right then Miss Titties would always be his secret name for her. 2Day could laugh at it. Now.

"Don't ever leave me, Clarkless. I mean it. If New York proves anything to us, it's that we *belong* together. Everything we do makes sense. Our souls have like a resonance. I'm not talking about some *fag et hag* shit, I mean just, just don't ever run off and leave me the way Alex did to Annette. Will you promise me that?" 2Day was unsure where this was coming from within her. She looked at Clarkless then, took all of him in; in one deep, hard breath like an excellent hit of ice. She wanted to hold him in her lungs forever, never come down. He smiled, the smile everyone else thought was mocking. And with everyone else it usually was. He reached up and tweaked her tit.

"Never even thought about, Miss Tittykins. What would I do without you? And besides, Alex is a..." Clarkless paused, expression pensive. Made a clucking noise with his tongue, a kind of glottal stop-pop which Southern drag queens and transsexuals affected. "Well, *whatever* he is, I will never, EVER, be like him. And you, my dear, will *never* be like Annette."

Comforted, 2Day reached over and flicked Clarkless across the balls. He jumped back, crashed unwittingly into Amber. They both fell to the ground with indignant squeals.

"You whore-faced cockmaster!" Clarkless yelled at her while clutching his crotch. Laughing, he pulled first himself, and then, with considerable effort, Amber up.

2Day giggled.

"So, what did you think about Trevie now that you finally got a piece of him?" 2Day asked, already sure of the answer.

"Oh. MY. *GOD*," Clarkless breathed. "His dick is monstrous! No wonder he let the big girl take it." Amber was spinning again, out of earshot. Clarkless and 2Day laughed in her direction.

"It was better than I dreamed of. I mean his ass is so rock hard and his assho—"

"Ugh, perv-boy that's enough," 2Day said in mock outrage. "So, what IS our plan for today then? I have that performance tonight, but that's not until seven, or eight, I can't remember. Ams? What time is the thing?"

Amber ceased spinning and did a dance. A bumbling copy of what 2Day had been doing on the way to the subway station. She laughed and shouted as she danced. "Step! Ball change! Step! Ball change!" so loud it rang across the station, getting everyone's attention. The dark kids looked at Amber with apprehension and interest, while the old woman clutched her Filene's bag harder to her chest, stood up and shuffled away. Sensing a moment, Clarkless and 2Day grinned at one another. Began cavorting around, screaming, "Step! Ball change! Turn! TURN! TURN! TURN!" Amber followed the instructions, turning herself around until she fell down again. After they stopped laughing, 2Day and Clarkless helped the girl up.

"OK, seriously? No more falling. I'm gonna need to hit a bowl again before I lift you up, Princess Fiona," Clarkless said. Ordinarily such a comment would make Amber pissy, but she was too high. Likely higher than she had ever been, so she just laughed the fall off. 2Day laughed harder, especially since Clarkless had used aloud their secret nickname for Amber. The girl did look like a white-painted version of the cartoon ogress from *Shrek.* But 2Day was somewhat mortified Clarkless had said it aloud.

"What did you mean?" 2Day said to Clarkless, once Amber flitted off to turn again in stupid circles, "that I will never be like Annette?"

They both had liked Annette—but *everyone* liked Annette. She was the essence of a social butterfly, easygoing, fun, funny and pretty. The woman had a natural ability to network. Whether at a party, a concert, a rave, or in an office. It was uncanny, seeing as how everyone in Annette's family all but hated her for one reason or another. Yet both Annette and

Alex had been role models of a sort in the rave and party circles around Southern Louisiana—a long time ago—when both Clarkless and 2Day were getting started in the scene. As a pair, Clarkless and 2Day had looked up to the other pair. Alex was as gay as Clarkless, only more mature and more experienced. Annette had been everything 2Day had wanted to be, at least on the surface.

2Day supposed it was inevitable that Clarkless and Alex began fucking each other. Alex was the man who had gotten Clarkless into meth. Clarkless then led 2Day to the drug. Annette was a pillhead—she didn't approve of meth—but "her Alex" could do no wrong. Their relationship seemed so concrete, so untouchable, their affection for one another surrounded by a solid wall nothing and no one could penetrate nor dismantle. And then, unannounced, Alex left. Disappeared. Alex left Clarkless, left Louisiana, *left Annette*. None of them knew where Alex went or why. Clarkless's NYC dreams, like the meth use, had their origin in Alex, who had whispered about his own dreams of living there. Of being the next big writer to tackle the city, to make it his own vibrant canvas. Clarkless was heartbroken. 2Day had been there to guide him through it. Meanwhile, Annette started a steady decline which ended with a hospital commitment and a total breakdown. Apparently she had always been a little crazy, which explained why her family was so cold to her. Still, it was hard to dissociate the episode from Alex's departure. Surely that had been the hardest and most potent shot in destroying whatever stability Annette had.

Clarkless grinned at her. "You're not crazy, for one, Tittymonster. And second, you're not in love with me like Annette was in love with Alex. Not in that way, at least. He used to talk about it a lot, about how smothered he felt around her. It was why he wouldn't let me get too close. He was afraid to care for people, because for him, at least he used to say—I'm not sure I believe it anymore—he used to say that caring for him was a commitment and he was bound to it once it reached a certain point. He couldn't just let go if things went bad. That he would just give of himself until there was nothing left to give and then *he* would be nothing." Clarkless shook his head in disbelief. "And then he ran. Supercilious bastard. Pretentious asshole. I dunno. 2Day, or Karen, or Miss Tittycaca, whatever your name is," Clarkless nudged her playfully, "I know that *I* don't *ever* wanna live without *you*."

2Day wiped her eyes, smearing the thick eyeliner. Clarkless laughed at her, hugged her. The sound of the train came blaring after the first push of stale tunnel air.

"Train's here! All aboard fags and hags and ogres!" Amber chanted. Clarkless gave 2Day a look. *Oh shit*, the look said. They both looked over at Amber and tried to smile as pleasantly as possible. But they both suddenly knew their friendship with her was over after today.

"So. What is the plan?" Amber said as they boarded the nearly empty 2 train. Amber was still doing the little dance she and 2Day were responsible for performing later in the evening. 2Day looked to Clarkless, though it was unnecessary. They knew each other well enough to already be on the same page. They had a plan, though neither had spoken it aloud yet.

Ditch. Amber.

Getting no response, Amber sidled up to them both and plopped down into the seat between them.

"So really, guys, what *is* the plan?"

Anton

East Village, Manhattan, New York City.

"Place in trying or constraining circumstances; distress; harass."

"Roasted peanuts!" the vendor cried, his waving arm somehow both bestial and sexual. Anton stumbled. Collided with a bit of just-below-the-waist-height iron fencing surrounding a square plot of dirt in the sidewalk, a tree growing amid the railing.

He had no idea what kind of tree. Who knew that kind of shit anyway? Anton wasn't sure *where* he was. Only that he was still somewhere in the East Village. Anton squinted, tried to adjust his vision. Took a few deep breaths, told himself he felt steady, could walk again. Reaching back, he felt around his asshole—outside of his dirty pants—checking to make sure he wasn't leaking.

It feels *dry.*

Still, he wasn't sure. His clothes were damp with sweat. They felt too tight, binding. He wanted to take them off. That guy, that fucker. Davis. The man had let him take a short shower, given him a bag of tina and the bottle of poppers. And told him to leave.

To fucking LEAVE. After I ate his SHIT.

Anton snarled. He had hoped to spend at least a few days at Davis's place, not doing *this* again. Walking the streets of Manhattan. In the dark of the night. So high he could barely see, so horny he could barely think. Not at all satiated and without a clue where to go. If he had known Davis would have freaked out so much Anton never would have asked about the man in the picture. Davis's reaction was like, well, Anton didn't know what it was like, couldn't know just then. He did know the reaction was fucked up and strange, seemed to have no reason behind it. They had been having such a good time, the guy had seemed so into it—into Anton—into *abusing* him. Davis had been good at it.

What a shady asshole.

Anton stumbled further down the block, an idea blooming in his mind. *The bathhouse.* This time of night, the place was bound to be open and busy. Anton didn't have any money, but they would let him in anyway, they *all* knew him by now. If only he could figure out where he was. Stumbling, Anton passed a Kinko's which looked vaguely familiar, and a diner which also looked like a washed out memory. An art gallery was next... until it occurred to Anton. *Everything looks familiar.* Vaguely. Despite all the concrete in those facades, none of the places seemed real. Anton still had no idea where he was. Pushing forward amid the shadow-soaked street, Anton made his way to an intersection, held hard onto the crosswalk sign as he looked up to read the street sign above.

"2nd Avenue," Anton read. Twisting, he looked up at the other, complementary sign. "13th street." Like bells going off in

Anton's brain, those street names collided and produced a response.

"*Square Pegs*," Anton mumbled. *It's somewhere near here... that's Union Square up ahead, right?*

What day is it?

Thoughts ran mad through Anton's brain. Little mini-movies of his evening with Chris. *No, his name was Davis.* Of the photo that had fucked it all up, the men printed on the paper composed of wavering hatch lines, as though artfully dawn in an purposefully messy animation. Anton tried to remember the name of the man in the photo with Davis.

Did I get the guy's name at least? Did I forget it?

I DID!

I did.

Anton remembered opening the picture's frame, the memory as broken and re-constituted as all his other memories, under the cloud of a meth high. His filthy, greasy, shit-stained fingers leaving grotesque brownish prints on the glass, the frame, and photo paper. Like the Marauder's Map in Harry Potter, scrawled text appeared to write itself across the back of the photo in Anton's memory. *The back of the photo had names written on it!*

And a date.

Fuck, what was it?

Light flooded Anton's soupy vision. He moved without thinking. Fell backwards onto the curb, the loud honk of a speeding cab seeming to come minutes after the car whizzed past, lights blinding. Blinking and rubbing at his eyes, Anton moved across the crosswalk. Heedless of whether he had the right-of-way, stumbling. He made it across, stepping up uneven onto to curb, nearly falling backwards again. His arms did a cartoonish windmill, correcting his balance just before a car passed lazily behind him through the intersection. But Anton wasn't able to pay proper attention.

"Fuck." A rush from the tina in his veins spiked through him, making him gyrate with *need*. He half-ran forward, his feet making sloshy smacking sounds against the pavement. He broke into the familiar space of Union Square like the opening scene to a fucked-up musical. A bright red *Virgin Records* sign shone above the street, next to that weird art-piece no one, least of all Anton, understood. Throngs of people milled about: Rasta-fried white kids, their nappy dreadlocks mussed and lank, their clothes drab, a few holding skateboards, like they were also an art installation no one understood anymore, if ever. A street performance anachronism. Not a thought Anton would ever have. He just tried to picture the shape of their bodies beneath their dirty clothes.

Beyond the peripatetic punks were a group of dark, bearded men dressed rather like clowns, screaming at a small crowd gathered around them. Their little three-pointed jester hats bobbed as they gesticulated and screamed, the bells on the tips of the hats tingling. Outside the doors of *Virgin Records*, an overdressed, disgruntled looking woman stood back from the crowd. She was flush against the brick facade, searching around in slow, steady arcs. Glaring at passersby as their faces rushed past, washed by the red glow of the *Virgin Records* sign. She wore a long coat. A navy blue pea-coat or something, too tight and too short. She was taller than Anton by at least four, maybe five, inches. Her jeans sported a visible muffin-top, which could be seen where the coat parted in the front. Anton considered asking her if she knew where "Square Pegs" was...

But why would she?

It was a gay-only bathhouse in a nondescript building, somewhere off Union Square. He was sure of that much. But no sign announced the place. If you didn't know it was there, didn't spot one of the leather-clad faggots going into that nondescript door, you might have no idea it existed. So there was no likelihood of the expectant woman knowing where the place was. Pushing the woman out of his thoughts, Anton decided to ask the first gay guy with whom he crossed paths.

Maybe he'll even go with me.

Roaming around the fringes of the Square—Anton wasn't sure how long, occasionally checking himself, paranoid that his ass was leaking again—Anton finally found a gay couple. An obvious muscle daddy and his thirty-something boy. Both of them wearing leather chaps, each cut different. "You guys know where Square Pegs is?" Anton asked, gyrating as another unexpected rush of tina surged through him.

The Daddy looked Anton up and down. Looked to the younger man—obviously Daddy's fuck-toy—and smiled. "Why do *you* wanna go there? That's a leather-pig fetish place. You're just a little twink."

Anton snarled at that word. Only stopping himself by the skin of his teeth from surging forward to attack the Daddy. The fuck-toy noticed and laughed. "I don't think Puppy likes being called a *twink*, Sir."

Sir. Yes. Fucking leather fags. Perfect! They HAD to know.

The older man nodded. "Well, we can take you there, puppy. But if we do... you gonna let Sir play with you?"

Anton didn't pause, didn't think, he just nodded, like a happy dog. Sir grinned. "I like this one, Alex."

That name hit Anton like a dickslap in the face. *That's the name of the guy in the picture! Fucking ALEX!* The last name had been on the picture as well, but that didn't come up in Anton's mind.

"You guys party?" Anton asked as they walked out of Union Square.

The older man, Sir, answered, "We do. But you *will* call me *Sir*." He said this with an inherent threat behind the words.

Anton nodded, "Yes, Sir."

This was going perfectly.

A man like this might take him back to a million dollar loft in TriBeCa. Maybe keep him as a live-in houseboy. Or a full-time sex slave and party favor. For weeks, maybe months—maybe *forever*. Anton's mind spun with possibilities. The trio had just passed back across 13th Street when Sir asked Anton, "What is Puppy's name?"

"Anton, Sir," Anton replied, having played this Daddy-Son game before. He knew it well.

Sir smiled. "Good boy."

"ANTON!" a voice shouted, confusing him. He spun around, wondering why Sir was shouting his name. Wondering if maybe he should run. Wondering what running would do to his already loosened, possibly leaking ass. "Anton!" the same voice said, only closer now, stressed, the sound of a shout from someone lightly jogging.

Of all people, *Prather* loped into Anton's view; looking aggravated and winded, wearing a bright-ass, yellow t-shirt with faded stars and writing on it, brown pants and boat shoes. No jacket. Despite the December chill in the air, it was unseasonably warm, if still cold enough he should have a jacket on. Prather glared at Anton, looked past him to the couple just beyond, to Sir and the new Alex.

"We've been looking. Everywhere. For you," Prather said, annoyed. Sir's eyes went wide and full of sudden fear.

"We didn't know... He said he was eighteen..." Sir said.

"Ugh. He's nineteen, actually," Prather said offhandedly to Sir. Prather focused on Anton. "Listen, Taty is worried fucking sick. You haven't called in weeks. She thought you might be dead. You need to stop, Anton. Whatever it is you're looking for... *this*," Prather waved at the couple, at the air in general, as if to say 'whatever you are doing now', "*this* is NOT it." Whatever it was, words failed Prather.

Anton reeled. Swayed on his feet, another surge of tina-high rocketed through him. "I'm busy, Prath. Unless you wanna come with." Anton directed a thoroughly nasty leer at Prather. It was the first time he had actively flirted with Prather in years. Maybe since that incident so long ago, when

Prather had so fully rejected him. When Anton was still just a little kid.

"I..." Prather seemed at a loss. Alex and Sir were moving away. Their faces showed they were clearly bothered. Too bothered, perhaps. Also maybe a bit unsure.

Anton swore under his breath. "Don't go, Sir. Please. I *need* it," Anton wailed.

Sir stopped, looked at Anton, eyes narrowed. "Are you *sure* he's nineteen?" The question was directed to Prather, who nodded in the affirmative, words still out of reach.

"Then, if the boy wants to go with us, that's up to *him*, isn't it?" Sir said sternly, flexing his arms. Prather sighed, words returned.

"Fine. Just call Taty? When you sober up. I'll tell her I saw you. She'll feel... better," Prather said, trying to assure Anton of something. Something of which Anton didn't need to be assured.

What is Taty to me anymore? The bitch is a fucking junkie hippie has-been artist who only cares to notice me when she has forgotten me long enough to feel truly guilty about it.

My leftover cocoon. Fuck her.

"Prather?" a woman's voice said. It was the girl from outside Virgin Records. Her face glowed, though the red light of the sign was far enough away it left her tinted. She must know Prather, Anton thought. Maybe even be in love with him.

Stupid bitch. He doesn't know how to love. Good luck.

"Jules?" Prather said, sounding harried. The handsome

man sighed and waved Anton off. "Promise me you'll call her."

Anton glared at Prather. The man was like family. For Anton, he *was* family. The very sense of the word had become so distorted by life with Taty and Vich that Anton's conception of family naturally included Prather, among others—and strangers who had somehow become *not* family.

Anton still wanted Prather sexually, even after all these years. Even after thinking of him as family. He felt wrong for it but the drugs made wrong *silly*. Outdated and not modern. What Anton really wanted right then was Prather to *take* him, shake him roughly. Grab a handful of Anton's hair, whisper meanly into his ear: that if Anton was going to call any man Sir, it damned well was going to be, him. Prather. But even fucked up as he was, Anton knew that was pure fantasy.

Prather doesn't see me that way. Never will.

But the man was more than capable of annoying Anton. Following him and tracking him down if he refused to offer the promise sought. Still glaring, first at Prather, then at the foolish girl, Anton said, "Fine. I promise." And for sheer spite, he ground out the next few words, in a shrill hateful tone. "I'll call when I get sober, DADDY," Anton said, laughing at Prather. Prather's eyes went wide. Anton got another rush.

I never got so much reaction out of him!

Score.

Prather nodded, turned towards Jules. Took her arm and said something low, close to her face. Something which made her give Anton a meaningful look before they turned away as one, walked towards Union Square. Anton was seemingly forgotten. Anton laughed, almost manic, as he looked back to see Sir and Alex impatiently staring at him. "Whatever *that* was all about..." Alex muttered. Alex's body pressed against his clothes and Anton noticed him fully for the first time.

He is really fucking hot—hotter than Sir. At least physically.

Sir had a bit of paunch over his thin hips and leg, under the wide slabs of pecs. But Alex was slender. And muscular. Brimming with the kind of near effortless svelteness of a man who was active and athletic as opposed to being only a gym rat.

He does some kind of CrossFit or something.

"C'mon then, boy. Square Pegs is just over there," Sir said, gesturing over towards a nondescript, unlit door. It looked like a shade of deep gray, recessed into a blank beige wall of bricks between two boutiques. All situated under rows of brownstones and townhouses which had likely been converted to small, ridiculously expensive apartments. Anton couldn't help himself, touched his asshole again over his pants, paranoid about leakage, but deliriously happy regardless.

"We don't have to go there if you guys don't want. I'm totally cool just going back to your place, playing with just you guys," Anton offered.

Sir shook his head. "Nope. We're gonna see just how far you'll go first. If you make Sir happy, maybe he'll take you home for *REAL* training." Sir's tone was still stern. Even a little sinister. But that could just be the drugs working on Anton.

Even Alex seemed to leer now. A sick, expectant grin splayed across his face.

"Yes... Sir," Anton said, adding the "sir" a half-second late.

Jules

Union Square, Manhattan, New York City.

"To advance upon vigorously."

"*That* was *really* strange..." Jules said as she and Prather walked back into Union Square. Back towards *Virgin Records*. Her comment was more of a question, the kind of undercover question she liked to ask without really asking. Always hoping not to seem to be prying. Prather just nodded at her, offering up nothing.

"So," Jules said, trying to fill the gap, "you said you *had* to see me..." She couldn't keep it out of her voice. The hope. The need. Prather was still arm in arm with her. *He's radiating something.* Only it wasn't warmth. It was *hot,* but not warm. In the same way habanero peppers were hot, but not warm.

It's a sense of purpose, maybe...

Prather *knew.* Not just who *he* was—who he *is.* So confident, so secure. He *knew* his own trajectory. Aimed himself with such exquisite precision. Jules wanted to mount him right there, in public. Part of her also couldn't wait to dish about Prather to Davis. To get his foolish, oddly wise ideas, his skewed point of view. She flirted with the idea of popping in on him, though she knew he hated that. She *was* only three blocks from his place.

Shit, Make that four.

"I didn't say that. I said I was *hoping* to see you," Prather said, soft.

What the fuck?

Jules stiffened and tried to cover it. But Prather still pulled away from her.

"It's OK, Jules. I just wanted to be clear. I know you'll appreciate that," Prather said.

Jules nodded. Had they talked about that? It was all such a whirlwind. Prather felt like the Bad Seed all over again, like that night she had smiled so much her cheeks hurt the next day. She had been almost unable to talk. Hadn't she just thought about how much she wanted him, for his precision? Could she fault him?

No.

She relaxed.

"It's fine, really. I was just... never mind. Forget about it, please?" She smiled at him. He looked unsure for a moment, then nodded.

"So..." Jules started to say, about to ask him where they were headed. But Prather seemed to sense her errant thoughts.

"Let's go back to your place. We should get off the street," Prather said. He didn't say *why* they should get off the street. Jules did not care. Her place sounded fine. But her thoughts strayed to Davis. They had to pass Davis's building on the way. She couldn't get the idea of stopping by to show off Prather to him out of her head. It annoyed her to be so unsure about it. *Aren't we supposed to be each other's best friend? Closest confidantes? Most important people in each other's lives? Davis should want to know about Prather, for fuck's sake...*

He could be the ONE.

Again, Prather sensed something going on in her mind. "What is it? Do you not want me to come over?" Prather asked.

"No! NO," Jules said. When Prather blinked at her she quickly added, "I mean, *yes.* I do. But, it's just, well, we're gonna pass by my best friend's building on the way. And I thought maybe we could pop in. You know, say hi."

She glued her eyes to Prather's face, eager to gauge his reaction. Curious to see if he would reject the notion. His face gave nothing away, but he did agree.

"If you want."

Jules beamed. She briefly thought of calling Davis first. But she rejected that, knowing he would just tell her he was busy or some other bullshit lie. Likely all he was doing was trolling online on one of those gay hookup things for a late night fuck session.

"Dick for every minute of the day," Davis had once said in regards to the app. Grindr. And Scruffed or something like that. Maybe both. And others.

"Lemme just see..." Jules said, fishing out her phone and looking up Davis on Facebook. His last post was a few days before. She texted him and got an automated response she knew well. *"Greasy hands!"* Shit, that meant he had someone over and couldn't use his phone, but it could also mean he had just forgotten to turn the auto-responder off. Jules knew

115

another way to find out. Davis would kill her if she ever admitted to it. She logged into Grindr, her faked user profile showing a full cadre of unread messages. *If all those dick-hungry faggots knew I had a pussy, they'd run screaming!* She snickered, navigated to her Favorites list and found what she was looking for. Davis's profile, the status light green, indicating he was looking to hook-up. It likely also meant he was alone. She logged off Grindr and put her phone away.

"OK. He's home, let's go," Jules said companionably to Prather. He nodded at her again, but he did not take her arm.

"What is your friend's name?" Prather asked.

"Davis," Jules said, the name drifting sweet off her tongue.

Prather looked as if he recognized the name.

Of course I must have told him all about Davis.

"You mentioned him a lot the other night. You seemed to think he was pulling away from you. Are you sure he will want us around?"

"We won't be staying long and of course he will. He's like my first husband. The best friend I've ever had. We love each other, even if we've grown a bit apart. I think he'll want to meet you..." Jules said.

And want to fuck you no doubt!

Prather looked at her, expressionless. Jules cringed inwardly, annoyed she had said that. *Fuck!* "What makes you say that?" he said, jumping right on her comment.

"I..." Jules began to stutter, trying to think fast. Think of something that was far from the possible truth: that she was pretty sure she had already fallen for Prather. That she wanted him as hard and strong as she had ever wanted anyone, the Bad Seed included. More, she felt a *connection* between the two of them, already formed; an ethereal, invisible line, but one which tugged at her, like an incessant need, a cold hunger. She knew telling a man that, showing her *need* to a man—even one as amazing as Prather, as deep and honest and precise— would make him run. There was no doubt in her mind. Life had taught her that. Painfully.

"I..." she said again. "It's just... you're an *artist,* and you live such a Bohemian lifestyle, and you have such a crazy scene around you. Like that kid we just left, what was his name?" She hoped he would take the diversion. It was weak and she knew it, but she was grasping. Desperate. If he cottoned to her true feelings... She made herself not think of that.

"Anton. He's my house-mate's kid. I wouldn't say I have a *crazy* scene around me, but Bohemian? That's almost condescending, Jules," Prather said, though his tone betrayed nothing. No anger, consternation, affront, approbation; *nothing.* Jules opened her mouth then closed it, feeling trapped and confused. Totally unsure what to say next.

"I..." Jules started, looked away. Prather put a hand on her shoulder. "It's OK, Jules, I didn't mean, I didn't take it *that* way. I'm sure you didn't mean it that way."

Jules anxiously straightened her pea-coat, unsure exactly what she *had* meant. Because nothing had seemed offensive to her in the comment, nothing at all condescending, but it must be. Prather said so.

How can calling someone Bohemian be condescending when I

meant it as a compliment?

She thought about it harder. Supposed it didn't *have* to be a compliment that she was attracted to that freewheeling aspect, what she would term Bohemian. After all, she could never live that way, didn't understand how others did, even if she did occasionally find such a man incredibly attractive. Wasn't the insult that she had to qualify it at all? It was just life to Prather. Jules winced.

"I didn't," she hedged, hoping it would die there. Prather gave the ghost of a sigh and leaned towards walking on. They moved towards Davis's building. The walk didn't take long. Soon they were outside the six-story converted brownstone, pushing the intercom buzzer for apartment 6B.

No answer.

Jules leaned on the buzzer again, and still no answer. But then without any voice coming on the opening buzz sounded, the maglock on the door released. Jules smiled at Prather as she led him inside. They climbed the stairs, Prather always a step behind. As she passed each floor her smile widened with expectation. Davis would know what it meant that she had brought Prather over; she wouldn't have to say anything. She was already preparing herself to take in her best friend's first look, knowing it would be the purest evaluation she would get.

She smoothed her brownish hair, straightened her coat (though it didn't need straightening), and adjusted her jeans. Her favorite jeans, which made her ass look amazing even if they did give her a *slight* muffin-top.

Very slight.

Once they reached the sixth floor, Jules was shaking with happy nerves, aware she hadn't seen Davis for a few weeks now despite the fact that they usually made plans every week. And that she had something way momentous to present to him. Jules tapped loudly on Davis's door. She could hear footsteps inside, coming close to the door. They stopped. But the door didn't open.

Shit. He must have looked through the peephole.

More footsteps and, weirdly, fantastically, the door opened.

There was Davis, his muscles slick with sweat, wearing only a pair of very low cut boxer briefs, hair tousled and expression a bit blank. She couldn't help herself, Jules' eyes wandered to Davis's crotch—his enormous hard-on was there, like a long shelf installed just above his balls, extending to the edge of his left hip.

"What the...?" Davis said, fazed. "Jules?"

Jules smiled and swallowed. She leaned in to move into the apartment, but Davis still stood casually barring the way. He had never done that before. It felt odd that, along with *not* having a key, Davis had refused to give her one when he moved to this place, saying he didn't want her walking in on an orgy or anything. She could see candles burning in his living room and heard low techno music playing, but she didn't see signs of anyone else in the place.

"What's UP?" she finally managed to get out, not looking back at Prather, sure if she saw his face she would freak the fuck out wondering what he was thinking. It occurred to Jules she hadn't introduced Prather yet, even though Davis could clearly see the man. Was in fact checking him out, up and down.

"A present?" Davis asked. He grinned lasciviously at Prather. *"Just* what I wanted..."

Then Jules knew. Together with his sweaty face, sallow skin, leering expression, and hypersexual posturing, it painted a picture in Jules' mind more clear and evocative than Prather could have managed to create.

He's high. Crazy high. Fuck, Davis.

He might be alone, but if he was, and that was definitely an if, it was recent. She could almost smell sex underneath whatever scent those candles spewed.

"Not quite." Jules sighed. She did not like dealing with Davis when he was high. He never smoked that meth shit around her, knew too well she more than did not approve — she was appalled by it. Davis had confessed his meth use to her after they had moved to New York together, in their first monumental fight after the move north. During that argument, Davis had blamed her for everything, including his drug use. Telling her he had never done drugs before he met her, before *she* had given him that pill of ecstasy at that rave.

"Not that I blame you or anything, Jules..."

Who would even say something like that unless they actually did blame you?

Fuck that was a long time ago.

She had not believed him then. He had always bragged about doing LSD and ecstasy, claimed to have started it as far back as the ninth grade. Jules had assumed Davis was an expert on something as tame as esctasy. He cried when he told her his stories about drug use in high school were all lies. Just like his claim to have slept with a woman. Something else he had never done before he met her. That fight had degenerated into something else entirely. Something neither of them had wanted, nor expected. Still, it had *ended* well. With hugs and promises, stroking of hair, and listening to Tori Amos, Stardust, BT while looking at pictures. At that moment it had felt like the rightest thing Jules had ever known. Even more than what she had thought she felt—no, what she HAD felt—with the Bad Seed. That the Bad Seed had been a lie wrapped in another, crueler lie didn't invalidate her feelings, make them any less real. Only pointless and irrelevant.

"Davis... I wanted to... I mean, we were just down the block. I figured you'd be around, thought we'd stop by and say hello. Since I hadn't seen you in a while. And I wanted you to meet... um. This is Prather." Jules thought her voice sounded ridiculous. Like she was high-pitched and babbling. Worse, as crazy as the thought might be, she felt like she was showing off a new boyfriend to a completely disinterested ex. One who had become less a friend and more of a frenemy, one who was cutting and cruel, but always couched under the cover of friendship. Jules' heart rebelled at that thought.

I can't feel that way with Davis!

What the FUCK?

"Um. Yeah. Nice to meet you. Prader," Davis said, smirking but not dropping his clear annoyance at the unexpected presence of his supposed best friend and a strange, if beautiful man. "He's *gorg,* Jules. But I'm kinda busy, you know..." Davis jerked his head towards the inside of his apartment. "I have someone coming over and I need to finish getting ready. Just had a twink here and he really messed the place up." For some reason Davis laughed. It took Jules a moment to remember what a twink was. Not that it mattered. Jules noticed something odd. Davis had an actual photograph in his hands. A photograph Jules knew *very* well.

"What... why are you holding that?" Jules asked, pointing to the photo. Davis looked at it as though he had forgotten it remained in his hands. It was slightly crumpled and had a few light brown smudges on it. Jules fixated on those muted brown marks.

Is that...?

Davis caught the line of her sight and his face veered to angry. He waved her question off, ending her unspoken supposition about what those stains might be. Jules remembered Davis mentioning he had seen Alex's father earlier. *In bad, old lady drag, no less.* Of course, that would make Davis think of Alex. Get him wondering about that asshole; where Alex was, what Alex was up to, whom Alex was fucking over now. *But walking around with the fuckshit's photo?* It was weird and gross to Jules. She had watched Davis become a different, worse person because of his connection with Alex. Because of the long and concentrated amount time the two guys had spent together. For her, too much of Davis's identity was wrapped up in some kind of reaction rooted in

Alex.

"We should go, Jules..." Prather said. She had interrupted him before he could respond to Davis. If Davis's attitude, leering appraisal, or dress had bothered Prather, Jules divined no indication when she turned to look at him. Prather was calm incarnate.

"The... I dunno, Jules. The kid who was just here. Um, reminded me of Al... *of him.* Then after seeing Mr. Richardson earlier... Maybe I just miss him. Despite what he did, despite it all. Maybe he *was* the one for me. Maybe if I had him I wouldn't be standing here sweaty and high and horny and... misera..." Davis's mouth snapped shut. Jules blinked, her calm shattered. She could not believe he had said any of that. Davis *never* admitted stuff like that. *Never.* And now he had done so in front of a total stranger. Jules longed to reach out to him, take him in her arms, despite whatever *that substance* was glistening on his body. *I hope it's not Crisco. Again.* Instead, Jules settled for a comforting smile. "There's nothing wrong with that, Davis. You should know that... I?" Words failed Jules.

"Maybe I do. I dunno. Whatever." Davis moved out of the way, hung with one arm against the door. "If you wanna come in, you can. No one is coming over. I was just sitting around trolling online, recovering from my last session." Davis moved aside and waved them in.

Jules realized she had completely forgotten to gauge Davis's full reaction to Prather, other than the leering. She and Prather sat on the sofa while Davis went to put on a t-shirt and some sweats. Jules inched closer to Prather, who obligingly put his arm around her. When he returned, Davis sat on the loveseat facing the sofa. His apartment was dimly lit, with no overhead lighting anywhere. There was just one floor lamp, tucked away in the corner, its shade black and pointing light only down, as Davis had the top of the shade's cone covered. The music had stopped. Davis must have turned it off while he got dressed. Candles still burned, giving the mod-decorated space a wavering feel, intimate and yet not. Some of it Jules didn't recognize, had never seen before. A few of the framed pieces on the wall, the chair next to the sofa, the new coffee table, the flat screen TV on the wall. All of that was new, had arrived since the last time she had been inside.

"So, Prader..." Davis started.

"PraTHer," Jules corrected, "with a T H."

Davis sighed and smirked."Prather, then. How did you meet my Jules?"

Jules warmed somewhat. She loved when Davis called her "my Jules." It had been too long since he had done so. Still, the entire moment was surreal: sitting in his apartment with Prather, Davis high but refraining from smoking more, opening up and spending unplanned time with Jules, even if it *was* slightly forced. It was also surreal that Davis was even bothering to entertain her, rather than more pointless hooking up. They started talking.

Prather told, briefly, about how he and Jules met. Jules had been setting up her jewelry stall at the Chelsea Flea Market and Prather had been taking down his adjacent stall, which had been full of his paintings. They began talking about their respective crafts. Complimented one another on the other's work. Sensing something she couldn't articulate then—something about Prather beyond his amazing good looks and ease of conversation, something which assured her she wanted him—Jules asked him to come back to her place for dinner.

"She made me green bean casserole. I had never heard of it before. It was... surprising," Prather said, finishing.

Jules laughed. Davis was very aware of her green bean casserole. She had made it for him the first time she cooked for him. *What does he mean, surprising?* Prather had eaten his whole helping, but had not asked for more. She had thought he was just not a big eater. He was very skinny, after all. The question started to form, the necessity of knowing whether he had liked the casserole. It was part of who she was, cooking that dish for people. If Prather hadn't liked it, Jules did not think she could avoid such a terrible omen.

"It was tasty, just too rich to eat more than a bit," Prather added, without looking at her, addressing Davis. Davis snickered.

"I eat the whole pan whenever she makes it," Davis said through his snicker. Jules was relieved. Like some unseen agency had obligingly pushed air out of her.

"So. Are you two... dating?" Davis asked, fidgeting with the string of his sweatpants, addressing his question to Prather. Jules knew Davis had asked it for her benefit. He was like that, sometimes. It was another reason why she had to love him.

Prather looked uncertain. But the tone of his response was even and strong. "No."

Jules felt stunned. Her body stiffened under Prather's arm and he glanced down at her. She didn't look at him, unsure what she would say, unsure she could keep a check on her words. If she opened her mouth right then, there was no telling what might rush out, unchecked, unfiltered. And Prather was not finished. Davis arched an eyebrow and gave Jules a curious look.

Maybe he isn't as high as I thought.

"We've only been out the one time. Aside from now, that is. I can't think of it as dating. We haven't been on anything resembling a date yet," Prather said, and, maddeningly, his tone did not say whether that was a good thing or not. Still, it was all true. Jules was again reminded of how precise Prather tended to be. How honest. Brutally so, it might seem. She knew she could think about it deeper, if she chose. Find that maybe Prather's truth was actually not brutal at all. To Jules, brutal honesty was being both honest *and* insightfully cruel at the same time. If someone looked fat in an outfit, there was no reason to tell them so while listing the details of other failures as well, as if it were all part of the same diagnosis. By that standard, Prather was refreshing in his honesty. Real. Though Jules hated the way that word was so often used in describing a personality.

She nodded at Davis, trying to keep her emotions under control. This relaxed her a bit. Davis's being in her personal space was that comforting, regardless of any tension between them. Prather's arm squeezed her, letting her know he was aware he had made her stiffen. But he offered no other, further encouragement. Strangely, this stirred something within Jules, excited her. A large part of her wanted Prather to gush, to say he wanted those future dates. Wanted more of *her*, more of *everything*.

"Well, if I know Jules, then once you've had the casserole and been to her place, you've had sex," Davis said, giving her a stern look. "And I want to know... you look like an experienced guy. Answer something for me." Davis leaned in, leering with a grosser detail than any Jules had ever seen from him. It was lurid and glaring, like the feeling of being surreptitiously watched and discovering someone actually staring back at you. "How was the head?"

Jules laughed, her tension at Davis's leering evaporated. Still, she glared at Davis. They once had a semi-serious argument over which of them gave better head. Their techniques differed sharply. They had yet to find a test subject who would let them solve the debate for good, beyond anecdotal claims to superiority. Davis usually waited a bit longer before interjecting this bit—waited to know her current *whatever* longer. But then Jules remembered how Davis had looked at Prather upon first arriving.

Suddenly Jules was nervous. Prather had admitted to Jules he was bisexual. Admitted to having few distinctions or lines about sex—though he preferred women.

Fuck.

127

She joked about the head thing sometimes with Davis, but she had no desire to actually do it. And never with Prather. *What if he picks Davis over me? What if he actually went through with it in the first place? Could I look at him the same way? Would I be able to trust Prather around Davis after that? Or vice-versa?* She scowled, unable to stop herself, almost unaware she was doing it.

"The head was... enjoyable," Prather said. "I've had experience enough to know it is not technique which matters per se, but the desire to enjoy the act which makes sex great."

Jules glared at Davis, who laughed at her before he nodded appreciatively at Prather. She could tell now, tell that Davis approved, at least provisionally, of Prather. A feeling rose in her. Part nostalgia, part excited hope. From being in Davis's space, comfortable and not arguing, no pressure, being open and all of it. With *these* men: her Davis and this fantastic new addition to her heart, Prather. This was what she wanted, had always envisioned in her friendship with Davis. And had never been able to articulate during their arguments. Instead she would eviscerate Davis for not understanding. Until he would shout at her, "What the fuck do you *WANT* from me, Jules?"

But she didn't say anything. Instead silently marked the moment in her memory. She would blog about it later on her secret LiveJournal. As if her grand realization had been the high point—the denouement of their interaction—Prather pulled his arm from around her and said:

"Well, it was good to meet you Davis. Jules, don't you

128

think it's time we left?"

Davis

Union Square, Manhattan, New York City.

"To lay stress upon; emphasize"

His hands pressed to his stomach, Davis exhaled sharply. The sounds of footsteps descending the stairs outside his apartment echoed between his ears. A paranoid cacophony. Though he had not expected Jules to just show up—*Tori Christ, it was almost midnight now*—maybe he should have. He had been blowing her off for something like a few weeks now.

And that guy, he's so wrong for her. But so fucking hot.

So confident and calm while he just *sat* there. Appearing wise and collected—radiating gorgeousness—as though *nothing* could ruffle him. Davis had flirted, even knowing it would make Jules mad. How could he not?

Serves her right for showing up like that. She knows I hate that.

For all Jules knew, he could have been in the middle of something. Could have been expecting a trick. Could have opened the door naked instead of only in underwear, his hard dick thrown out there like a welcome mat. Hadn't he made sure to set up that automated text reply just to appease Jules? He'd even used the code words he had told her would mean he was busy. Still, he did use them all the time. It was not shocking that Jules would eventually begin to ignore them entirely.

Once he was sure they were actually gone, Davis walked over to the windows. He looked down at the street, waiting to see the couple emerge from the building.

That guy is so wrong for her, how can she not see it?

To Davis, Jules was erratic. Borderline nutballs, full on crazysauce at times. And this guy, this Prather, he was... well, he just *wasn't*. Maybe the guy knew that about Jules and was OK with it. In that case, maybe he *was* the guy for her. Clearly she thought of him that way, or she would not have brought him over. Especially not now, at this time of night. She wanted to show him off.

Classic Jules.

Well, whatever. I wish her well. Maybe if she has a guy she won't pressure me so fucking much.

Davis loved her. But shit it was a lot of maintenance being *so* important to someone *so* high strung.

The couple emerged from his building's front door, six stories down, arms looped together. Well, that was kind of sweet. It reminded Davis of what he had been doing before Jules surprised him.

Leaving the window, Davis went back to his bedroom, picked up the photo of Alex he had left on a table in the little hallway between the living room and the bedroom. He thumbed it with exaggerated care.

Why did I react that way to the little twink fucker? Why did I throw him out earlier? Alex isn't his fault. He doesn't even know *Alex.*

Sighing, Davis tried to think it through as he sat down in

front of his computer to check his email. Seeing none he switched to his phone to check Grindr, Scruff, Adam4Adam, and Jackd. He didn't feel like having anyone else over, but also didn't want to discount the possibility of someone really hot messaging him and inviting him to their place. Davis felt he might be up for that.

He knew what part of it was. Seeing Alex's dad, Mr. Richardson, had put Alex back in the front of Davis's brain. Alex himself never really left it. Davis thought about the man several times a day, on a good day. He would berate himself for it, try to stop, only to have those thoughts creep back in, mostly unwanted. And—when he believed he had forgotten about Alex for a while, like when his mind had been so wrapped up in punishing that fucking twink, the one who looked so much like Davis himself had years ago—to have that kid bring Alex *back* into his mind had been too much.

He shouldn't feel bad for kicking the fucker out. After all, Davis did let the twink shower first and gave him enough tina for a day, maybe two. Davis only had a gram or so left now; he would definitely have to go see Pritchard again after his next hook-up. Whomever that was. They would almost certainly want to use the tina; everyone did these days, except Davis. Not that he was opposed to it, it just didn't feel right most of the time. Worse, it made his emotions go all out of whack, brought out unwanted insecurities. Lowered what remaining inhibitions he possessed. But mostly, it made Davis want—*no not want; need*—Alex.

Fuck that.

Nothing worth pursuing on Grindr. Or Scruff. The same old faces, desperately trying to escape the little boxes in the app which contained them. All of them hoping someone would see more than that little square of flesh. Want more. They never did.

So fucking stupid.

Same on all the other apps. Lots of messages, but not one the level of perversion Davis needed to fill his Alex-void.

Davis sighed and stretched his arms out wide. He stood up and took off his sweats and t-shirt. Sleep would have been nice—but that wasn't going to happen, not yet—he was still too wound up from the twink. Tired, worn, but not quite chilled-out enough to crash. He could work on that new script he had been pitching to the programming guy from Bravo that he had been dominating on Thursdays. The same one Davis had fucked nearly unconscious using a baseball bat. The one who had read Davis's work online after their hookup, had emailed him with what seemed promising propositions.

But fuck, who am I kidding?

Davis wanted to be a creative guy, wanted something other than the easy money which came from understanding what a multidimensional array was, how data tables interacted, how SQL was properly parsed down to the kernel level. But just wanting that creative outlet didn't mean Davis would get it, or that he deserved it. Alex had told him repeatedly how talented he was, and Davis had believed it every time.

And look at Alex now.

A best-selling fucking author.

But that had been *love* talking. Alex had known what he was talking about—writing was Alex's thing, had always been his thing. He was so good at it that Davis always felt like a child grasping his father's tools in comparison. Yet even then, Alex had praised Davis's stories.

Concise. Driven. Gritty.

Those were the words Alex had used.

Davis had not been able to return the favor. Alex's stuff had been near indescribable attempts at what he called meta-fiction. Hypertextual stuff which Davis could not follow in a straight path no matter how he tried. It still boggled Davis's mind Alex could write the stuff at all. That had been over fifteen years in the past—when most people had no clue what hypertext was.

Even more damning: Alex had made a career, had succeeded and left everyone behind; fashioned something magical out of a gift which he did little to nothing to earn or develop. *He was just fucking gifted with it. The bastard.* Davis snarled, unable to stop himself.

It felt so personal the first time Davis saw one of Alex's books on a bookshelf at Barnes & Noble. Had also felt like a violation for Davis to get his first sight of one Alex's books on a shelf and not from Alex himself. The first time he heard Alex interviewed on *Fresh Air* was also the first time Davis had heard Alex's voice in years. It nearly destroyed Davis when he first saw Alex's name on short lists for literary prizes. As though Alex were standing next to Davis only to emphasize his relative success and thereby highlight the lack of it in everyone whom he had left behind. Davis was pretty sure he was not the only one Alex had abandoned. Being pretty sure certainly did not make him feel any better. Seeing Mr. Richardson only confirmed that yet again. Davis wondered if Alex even bothered to contact his Mom—they had been close —but it was likely even Miss Cathy had been dropped like everyone else. Somehow that supposition felt right—the idea, at least. The reality was simply disheartening and hurtful. Davis had adored Miss Cathy and the feeling had been mutual. Despite her disapproval of Alex's sexuality and their relationship in general, she had returned his adoration. She always insisted Davis have dinner with their family, as though he belonged there.

Whatever. That's done. That Alex is dead.

Davis started to crumple the photo up—unaware he was holding it again. His mind was far away, lost in memory.

Why can't I let Alex go?

It wasn't the writing. The success. Not any of it. It couldn't be. Davis was rich himself. Had inherited a fucking shitload when his Mom died. Enough to buy this apartment and pay the maintenance for the rest of his life and then some. Not to mention his regularly clearing over a hundred grand a year as a Systems Architect since moving to NYC.

No, it isn't a money thing. And success?

So what if Alex was published? Acclaimed, and touted?

Davis's dreams of being a "creative guy" had been just that: dreams. Something he wanted but never expected to have. So he had talent. Some, anyway, at least. It wasn't what drove his life, not like it had been for Alex.

So what the fuck is it? Davis snarled in thoughts.

Love? Can it be so fucking simple? That I loved Alex first? Most? Hardest?

Alex had also taught him sex could be more than just liberating. It could be enlightening, transcendent, recombinant with Destiny itself. Even when it was humiliating. That realization had carried over into other parts of Davis's life. Had taught him people could never beat you down for things you took into yourself, things you wore proudly, no matter what they thought of those things. Maybe it was just that he had believed Alex felt the same way about him. As Davis had so clearly, so confessionally, felt for Alex. Davis had meant it. Alex had not.

Clearly had not.

There was no way Alex was sitting around—wherever he was—dwelling on a photo of Davis, trying so hard to be wishing for something else.

Something more.

Maybe it was love, maybe it wasn't. Maybe Davis wasn't meant to understand it. Maybe he shouldn't even try. Davis put the photo down, turned it upside down, and looked at the back of it. The kid, that twink had looked at the back of it, had pulled the thing out of the frame before asking Davis about it. Was it possible the kid somehow knew Alex?

Why didn't I think of that before?

It made sense. Alex always had been a dominant top. He would have very much enjoyed using a kid like Anton. The same way he had used Davis, had taught Davis how to be used.

Had Alex somehow—of all the fucking twinks in New York City, had Alex taught this little fucker as well?

Davis reached over to ball up the photo again; angry, far more than he could rightly understand. He had been so much like that kid back then, only with the roles switched. Davis became the user, not the used—the abuser, after Alex left, months later—when he realized no matter how many times he contacted Alex, there would be no reply. When Alex's family, Annette, Jules, and everyone else had gotten the same, Davis had sunk into a depression which lasted for ten gruesome days. When he emerged—pounds lighter, lightheaded with sunlight and grief—he had felt like a butterfly. Like he had metamorphosed into something new, something Kafkaesque. Something *destined*. The next time he hooked up after awakening, Davis had become *rough, forceful,* and *demeaning.* Had discovered, however unintentionally, that guys, that pretty fags *loved* being humiliated. Seemed to crave it, even if they rarely admitted it, even after. It should have been obvious to Davis. After all, he himself had been one of those fags, had loved every inch and smack of Alex's sexual abuse. The feeling of strength which had invigorated Davis was like few other things he had ever known, aside from Alex. Unlike anything he had ever done before. It was then Davis had started building his body up, getting muscles and becoming the thick-set stud he was now. An image more closely matched to the new aspect of his personality—the new representation of his newly born self.

My post-Alex triumph.

That feeling had lasted some time, long enough to see him through to New York City. To overpower Jules' objections and convince her to follow him.

Had it all been a mistake, letting her follow?

Was it all his fault? Could it all be traced back to Alex? Would Davis feel haunted by that specter for the rest of his life? Was he going to spend all the years he had left trying to add up who he was against what Alex had taken from him when he left so abruptly? It was a horrifying thought, because Davis knew that particular abyss could never be filled.

Davis smoothed the slightly crumpled photo out. He decided right then not to destroy it. He knew, no matter how hard he tried, he could never eliminate his past from himself. Could never detach it, no matter how successful he had been at becoming something *else*. Something new; with wings and a shiny, protean body. Doing so would only highlight what he had lost. What was left behind, like a marquee of glittering, twinkling failure hanging over his head. Outshining everything else Davis tried to be, tried to do. It was futile, even symbolically. For some reason, Davis smiled at that thought.

Looking around the room, Davis sighed. He checked his hookup accounts again—every last one of them—but there was nothing new. He wished now he had not reacted so strongly to the twink fucker. That he had not sent the kid away so soon.

138

How many twinks are that perverted? He's like a unicorn or something.

Davis was still jacked up. Even though he was sober—he still had no desire to use tina—he was spun from the hours of play he and the twink had enjoyed. A loneliness, strong, needy, and vast, welled up within. Perhaps it had been there all along—a shadow which only now lengthened and became monstrous. The loneliness wracked his body like a seizure. His hands, hovering over the computer's keyboard, arched into nearly rigid claws. His vague reflection, shining and dissolved in the glass of the LCD monitor, glowed in front of his face, fuzzy and angry. His toes were curled, the nails dug hard into the fabric-like material of his flip-flops.

Funny. Of all the things he had been able to push out of himself, had been able to shed like old skin, loneliness was not one of them. Worse, the more sex Davis had, the more involved the play sessions became. And somehow, the more intense the play, the more lonely he was after, the more physically removed. There was something hidden in that knowledge, but just what eluded him. He knew this was why some people took tina in the first place—to escape loneliness. Build up the feeling they felt they needed in order to put themselves out there for consumption. For the first time ever, Davis pondered doing tina. Smoking some meth. It wasn't like he had anything to lose in doing it, Alex had been able to use it all the time and still be successful. Davis knew, innately, he would never want to use it so often as Alex had.

Davis shook his head, images of the randoms he had

fucked burbling up, reminding him of what meth did to people. Whether they could see it—understand it—or not. It released them in so many ways and tied them so tightly in so many others. Davis already had something tied around his insides, binding him; there wasn't room for anything else. Pushing away from the computer desk and his tablet, he grabbed his phone, decided he needed to get out of the apartment. Wander around. He could log in to Grindr and maybe find a hookup that way—or a date. The way he was feeling, he might even agree to actually follow through with a real date.

He quickly got dressed. Less than fifteen minutes later he was walking down 13th street away from Union Square, his iPhone snug in his jeans pocket, set to vibrate if someone messaged him on Grindr. Davis had little luck with that particular app. He got lots of replies, but they always wanted to do something mundane, something vanilla: have a drink, see a movie, have dinner. When all Davis wanted was sex; filthy, no-strings attached sex. It had become pointless. He hadn't used the app seriously in some time. But this time of night, he didn't expect many people to be actively looking—if they were, he would come to them, vanilla or not.

And maybe turn one of them out.

Trying to push his thoughts in a different direction, Davis looked around at the buildings he passed, remembering his first time in New York City, his first time in the East Village. How the place seemed like a let-down and a come-on at once. Both valid—neither more seductive nor disappointing than

140

the other. The place lacked the magnetism Davis had expected it to have. He had not felt like he would be unhappy anywhere else, the way Alex had often talked about New York City as they lay in bed dreaming. But the city had *something*. At the time he moved to NYC, Davis hadn't a clue what it was, only that he wanted to know. To hold it and examine it— search for answers. He and Jules had gravitated towards the East Village from the off. It seemed like the only place in the city that wasn't a stereotype, but rather a stereotype of stereotypes.

The entire city disgorged bits of itself into the East Village. Mixing the whole panoply of people all together into an almost sentient work of performance art composed of lives, and sounds, and smells, and actual art; rimed with drugs and sex and soul. Nothing else in the City compared to the East Village. Not for Davis, at least. Jules had agreed, saying she felt the same, though Davis expected she may have just been humoring him. Sometimes you could not tell the difference with Jules, her desire to please could be overwhelming.

Strolling slowly past a dive bar, Davis spotted everything from drag queens to punks to urban lumberjacks and prig-nosed JAPs. It was *that* mix which attracted Davis. Made him forget the loneliness he continuously nursed, however temporarily. He was not sure why the swirling throng of freaks soothed him, why it felt natural, relaxing. But it did.

Davis looked away from the dive bar, walked faster. He was nearing Alphabet City, the next block over would be Avenue A. Alphabet City made him laugh, always reminded him of that moment just before Alex and he had so abruptly ended, when they had been watching that movie—*200 Cigarettes*—both of them so charmed by the two girls in the movie. From some ridiculous sounding place on Long Island called Ronkonkoma. Freaking out because they were lost in Alphabet City, afraid of some Street called Avenue B. He and Alex had joked that if—no, *when*—they moved to New York they would visit not just Avenue B, but the fabled Ronkonkoma as well. Well, Davis had done both—with Jules, of course, not Alex. Somehow the experience had not been nearly as fun as imagination would have had it be.

Still laughing, Davis turned down Avenue B, decided he would walk down to Houston Street. Turn back towards the West Village, walk all the way to Washington Square Park. And if he had not found a hookup by then, hopefully he would be tired from walking, tired enough to pass out, to forget his swirling loneliness. The streets slowly lowered in number until Davis crossed 2nd Street. A little bodega on the corner was still open, even in the late hour. It had to be past one in the morning. Precious few people were about. The area had the somber quiet of a Manhattan residential neighborhood. But under all those shadows was an imposed otherness, and Davis felt it. The whole area was flooded with it, a heartbeat of counter culture which could not be dissembled no matter how calm things seemed.

Unexpectedly—enough to startle Davis—his iPhone buzzed in his pocket. Pulling it out, he discovered a message on Grindr. Curious, even a little excited, he opened the app and read the message. He nearly dropped his phone when he recognized the photo attached to the message. He saw photos on dating apps before he read any messages. What was the point of reading a message from someone repulsive? Though he also sometimes read the message anyway, if only to mock the asshole sending it.

But this?

How to react? How to feel?

He had been stressing to himself that he could not destroy his past, could not detach himself from it. And now, here it was: alive, aware and nipping at him through a hook-up app. The darkened buildings around him swam, leaned in, threatening. He was dizzy, the lights from the little bodega flashing bright for no understandable reason. Davis stumbled to a stoop and levered himself against it as he read the message.

"Wow. You look hot. Wanna fuck?" the message read. It was simple, concise, to the point and forward. The exact way Davis preferred, but the picture attached to it... *was this a fucking a joke?* Davis tapped on the photo, enlarging it on his phone as if by doing so he could find some way to discredit it. To prove it inherently false, reveal it for the trickery it must be. He could not erase the feeling inside, even though that feeling had shoved aside his loneliness, for now. Replaced it with a vibrantly brown mix of hope, desire, despair, incredulity, and piercing melancholy.

He stared at a photo of Alex Richardson, arm in arm with Davis himself. The photo had been cropped at Davis's arm, showing nothing more than his right hand and forearm. It was the exact same photo Davis had nearly crumpled earlier in his apartment. Brown smudge stains and all.

What the fuck?

Trevie

East Flatbush, Brooklyn, New York City.

"To exert force upon; pressure."

"Yo. Seen my phone?" Trevie barked across the living room of his apartment, looking towards the two bedrooms. No response. Trevie paused and listened.

"Fuck me," Trevie murmured.

He knew someone was still back there. Fuckin' Tuesday had left only an hour before. She took those two douches with her. Trevie pursed his lip. The guy Tuesday had been with, Clark something, was not really a douche. But the girl, that Amber, she was douchetastic.

Holy fuck she was good at giving head...

Deep throat is deep throat, whatever.

Trevie heard a noise from the bedroom again. He had no idea who was back there, but *someone* was. Someone always was. He had grown used to it. Comforted even.

"Fuck me," Trevie said again, pulling himself languidly off the sofa. He traipsed around the living room, turning things over, searching for his phone. He glanced back towards the bedrooms when he heard another noise, a soft thud.

"Yo! Is my fuckin' phone back there?"

Again, no answer.

Annoyed, Trevie went to the spare bedroom, taking in the

sight of the television, the play bed, and his wall of porn. All juxtaposed against a sling hanging in the corner.

Next time I'm getting Tuesday in that bitch.

But there was no one there so he moved on to look into his room. He never quite knew what would be going on around him at any given time. Trevie had not been completely sober in who knew how long. A year, maybe? Two? But walking in on some seriously crazy shit in his own bedroom had happened more times than he remembered.

Gah. Anton is such a fuckin nasty lil fag.

After walking in enough times to shit he didn't *ever* want to get involved in, Trevie had developed a weird sense of caution about entering his own bedroom unannounced. He tended to sleep in the living room.

"Comin' in..." Trevie yelled down the hallway towards his room. The door was ajar. Sounds came from the room, loud enough to be heard over the jungle music coming from the wireless speakers in the other parts of the house. Whoever was in there had the speakers turned off. Was either listening to the TV or the computer or something.

When Trevie didn't hear a response he shrugged and went in. No one there. Feeling disoriented and a little amused, Trevie walked over to the computer and searched for the source of the clamor. A small window was playing a movie— some kind of gang-bang, faux lesbian porn. Trevie vaguely recognized it as part of his collection, but had no recollection of putting it on.

Maybe that ogre-twat Amber did it.

146

Fuckin' dyke.

Trevie clicked the X and ended the problem. The room went quiet, the low thrum of the music from the rest of the apartment drifted through the walls indistinctly.

"OK. Fuck. What was I...?" Trevie said trying to remember why he had come in here in the first place. He moved some things around on the computer desk until it came to him.

Phone!

It wasn't on the computer desk, the bed, the nightstand, or near the TV on the shelf. He even got down and looked around on the floor, laughing when he found a sizable shard of ice wedged between two slats of chipped floorboard. As he stood back up, dizzy, he heard another strange sound. At first it sounded like the music blasting from the other rooms, but then he recognized it.

My ring-tone!

Trying to trace the source of the tone, Trevie finally sat down on the bed, closed his eyes and took deep breaths. He felt a vibrating lump in the pocket of his jeans. Reaching in, he pulled out his phone.

Fuck, I need some sleep.

The display showed a missed call from Pritchard. Church bells rang in his mind as Trevie realized he was supposed to be making a delivery to Pritchard today.

Fuck fuck fuckity fuck!

Trevie stared for a moment at his phone, knowing there was a reason he had been searching for it. Something other than Pritchard.

That sweet, old faggot.

Trevie smiled at nothing, thinking of Pritchard. The guy had been doing meth—dealing it sideline for something like twenty years—and somehow, *who the fuck knew how*, had managed to be both productive *and* hedonistic the whole while. Trevie had peppered the guy with questions, trying to divine Pritch's secret, but he suspected even Pritchard himself didn't know. Or if he did he was guarding that shit like his last shard. Trevie could not help but adore the old queen for that alone.

He's like my hero or some shit.

Feeling the mild, pulsing weight in his hands, Trevie came back to his phone. Again a sudden feeling of church bells ringing.

Anton! Fuckin'shitballs.

Trevie scrolled around in the phone, found Anton's cell and called it up. No answer. Voicemail full. He sent a text.

Fuck. What to do now?

Well. Anton hasn't been over in weeks. Sure as fuckin' shit he's gettin' high somewhere. He's getting ice from somebody. Maybe Pritch's seen the little shit.

Trevie could tell Pritch and Anton knew each other, if not as well as Trevie knew both. They had definitely had some encounters, though Trevie didn't inquire about those as a rule. Not when it was Anton and it involved someone with whom Trevie did business. Pritch had been enough solid business to pay Trevie's rent for near seven years. Trevie had no desire to damage that relationship. Still, it couldn't hurt to ask.

"Yo. Pritch-dick," Trevie said, after making the call.

"*Trevor.* How *nice* to hear your voice," Pritchard said in that low growl he used when he was covering anger with politeness, "I assume you're nearing a point of coming over?"

Trevie twitched in frustration. The truth was he couldn't make the trip. He would need to get lit first. And that could lead anywhere. Maybe even to falling out. There was no use lying to Pritch.

"Nah. I'm way too lit man. I'm up on it and going through it, as it were," Trevie said, altering his voice at the last to mimic the tone of Pritchard's: fussy and low. As if he didn't need another distraction, Trevie suddenly wondered why everyone called Pritchard Pritchard. *Is that his first name? Or his last? Why haven't I ever thought of that before? And for that matter, how old is the guy? And where's he from? Did he just spring fully formed from some bathhouse?*

"I can come to you, Trevor dear. Will you promise to stay put for the next, say, two hours?" Pritchard asked calmly. *That's what I fuckin' love about this guy—nothing gets him really out of his shit!*

Again the church bells.

Maybe that's his secret. It's like maybe there's this store of shit in our brain. This max capacity of emotional output and by keeping his shit calm all the time Pritch never exceeds the max and therefore never loses his shit.

Beaming at the wall, elated with new insight, Trevie laughed.

"I'll take that oh-so-charming laugh for a concrete *yes*,"

Pritchard mumbled."Two hours, mind. Stay put, dear-heart."

"Wait. Pritch. Dude. Um, have you seen Anton around? Got mad people lookin' for the little turd banger," Trevie asked.

Silence.

Trevie was about to ask again, afraid the call had been dropped, when Pritchard made a throaty, discontented noise. "Ahem. Well, as a matter of course, I *have* seen the dear 'turd banger'," Trevie heard the inset quotations. "Just this afternoon." The words sent vibrations through Trevie.

What the fuck time is it? Is it still fuckin' Tuesday? Am I still fuckin' Tuesday?

Sidling back over to his computer Trevie looked at the date and time. Thursday. Five thirty-eight in the afternoon.

Fuck.

Somewhere he had lost a whole fuckin' day.

Man, whatever magic that Tuesday bitch has in her twat I need some more of it. Trevie laughed to himself. His mind reeled, knowing it was supposed to be focusing on something other than Tuesday's magical vagina.

Anton.

"Oh. Um. Yeah. You've seen him? Where?" Trevie asked.

"He came over today. With one of my regular customers, seeking party favors. I gave them my last—as I was expecting you. Hence the urgency of my call." Trevie wanted to laugh.

What the fuck? If this is urgency for Pritch, I would hate to see an actual fucking emergency.

"I suspect they are now, as we speak, reconvening at said

150

customer's penthouse. Engaging in all manner of unspeakable debauchery. They invited me to join them later. I am considering going. Would you like me to pass a message to dear Anton for you, then, should I decide to attend?"

Trevie blinked at the wall. He had a hard time following all of that. It took a few seconds after Pritchard stopped speaking before it all sank in.

"Um. OK. Yeah. YES! Give him a message. Tell him to call me or Prather or Taty. Like seriously, people need to hear from him. Mad cool of you, Pritch. So um, two hours? I'll be here."

"Fantastic," Pritchard said. "Will you be alone or should I expect to have to weave my way through a throng of sycophantic junkie neophytes? If so, I might need to rethink my outfit."

Trevie blinked at the wall again, patiently waiting for his mind to connect the dots of Pritch's words. Sure it would do so if he let it alone to do its thing.

More church bells. Trevie refused to listen to them this time.

"I..." Trevie stumbled, and it clicked. "Alone. Yeah, just me here." It was hard to know if Pritch was serious about changing his outfit, but it was entirely plausible. The faggot had shown up at Trevie's wearing ass-less chaps before. Granted they were shorts—very short shorts—but shorts conspicuously missing an ass. It had tickled Trevie, imagining the thick, buffed out queer walking through East Flatbush dressed so provocatively.

"Fantastic. I will see you shortly," Pritchard said but Trevie had already begun to pull the phone away from his ear, hanging up the call.

Well, at least I located Anton.

Squinting at his phone he called Prather. He wondered if Prather knew Pritchard, laughed lightly at the weird similarity in their names.

"Yes?" Prather answered. He sounded—not quite strained, Trevie couldn't put words to it—but in anyone else Trevie might have called it "moody."

Except Prather doesn't get fuckin' moody.

"Yo, Prath-dog. I found the little assgoblin. He was at my friend Pritchard's earlier this afternoon. Pritch is gonna give the people Anton is with a call and pass a message on to the little shit to call one of us."

"That's great, Trevie. I will text Taty and let her know. I am a bit... occupied at the moment, is there anything else?"

Trevie pulled the phone away from his face and stared at it in mock disgust. Even as blitzed as he was he could tell when he was being brushed off and, worse, being talked down to.

What the fuck, man?

"Whatever, P-dids. Nah, that's it. T-out," Trevie said, holding the phone directly in front of his mouth and shouting the last part. He tucked the phone into his pocket. The bedroom was now strangely silent and somehow *wrong*. Deviously empty. Trevie bounced a little on the bed trying to remember the last time he had slept in it. It didn't feel like his bed but rather like the bed of someone he knew well but had not seen in years. Someone he had run into accidentally only to end up staying over at their place. It only lasted a moment but he was disoriented by it. Worse, that he could not remember when he had actually slept in the damn bed was maddening. Trevie knew if he fixated on that line of thought any further he might get lost in such for days. He left the bedroom, comfortably ensconced himself on the sofa in the living room to wait for Pritch. Everything he needed was right at hand. Trevie sighed in relief. He did not feel dizzy anymore. He turned the music up until the boards in the sofa under him vibrated.

Fuck the neighbors, it's the middle of the fucking day.

Trevie loaded another bowl of meth, picking out an especially large shard, breaking off a pinky-tip sized chunk which he loaded into the water bong. He burned the bowl, sucked off the small amount of cut, let the glass cool. He enjoyed this moment. Particularly when he was alone. The ritual was engrossing. Trevie blew on the bowl, let the rush of his breath cool the molten ice until it hardened into a pale, crusty, yellow coating riming the bottom of the glass bowl. He set down the little torch and picked up the MAPP gas he kept sitting on the side of the sofa. Turning the safety off, he ignited the canister and burned the bowl in quick darting flashes, taking deep pulls. He held the flame directly on the bowl as he sucked in—until his vision swam and he could not hold anymore vapor. Trevie offed the MAPP gas and set it down carefully. Somehow managing to maintain those slow deliberate motions despite the feeling rushing through him as he exhaled. The cloud which swam out of his mouth was enormous. For a brief moment the whole of the living room seemed shrouded in nimble fog.

Still holding the bong Trevie stared at his reflection in the mirror across the room from the sofa. Eventually he fixated on the reflection of the bong itself. Unbidden, thoughts emerged.

When did this become the best moment of my life? When did the sum total of my joy become an object in a reflection? Does this mean I'm a fuckin' junkie? Does that label even really cover anyone these days? Fuck.

The word "junkie" always made him think of the movie *Trainspotting.* Of lanky, dirty Scots lounging about on a ratty, filthy floor screaming obscenities at the ceiling while the carpet rose up around them. Consumed them, leaving only hardly intelligible screams rebounding into nothingness. Trevie laughed, pleased by the depth of his thoughts. He set the bong down on the coffee table and wondered what his next step would be.

I don't wanna be a fucking dealer for the rest of my life. Until I get fuckin' busted or killed or overdose.

More need rose in Trevie. Familiar and insistent, full of questions and criticisms. The need had a voice he knew, yet somehow was not his own. The need was implacable, inching upward and out of his mind like vomit—like a cloud of leftover meth smoke—until Trevie leaned forward, glaring at the bong now only inches from his face. The rest of the room went out of focus. He spoke softly to it, sure it was listening.

"You don't own me, fucker."

But that *need,* and the accompanying voice, it scoffed at

him: "But I *am* you. BZZZZZZ"

Trevie's face jerked away from the bong as though it had reached out, burned him, and set off a buzzing in his brain like an electric shock. The room came back into focus as though he had, for a moment, been asleep, daydreaming.

"What the holy fuuuuuck," Trevie slurred. Without warning, the whole apartment went circular. The whole space was now like his bedroom: strange, unwelcoming, and unfamiliar. At the same time, he knew every bit of the space and was not at all afraid; part of him recognized the source of the feeling, the creeping influence of being awake for who-knew-how-fucking-long. Of being *so-fuckin-high*. Yet even with that knowledge, embalmed by the surety of it, the shadows around Trevie crept together, blobbing into one another and making lurid faces at him. Nothing seemed benign—even the bong itself was sinister, sitting there, mocking him.

Closing his eyes, Trevie sighed and took deep, long breaths. After all, it was not the first time he and the shadow people had relations, though he could not remember the last time it had happened. And those questions—the dire questions his need wanted answered—were still there. Hanging in the air around him like cartoon words in an after-school special with suffocating intent.

GET SOBER!

BE SOMEBODY!

GO TEAM!

YAY BOY SCOUTS!

ALL OUR BASE ARE BELONG TO US!

...

Is this what my life is going to be?

BZZZZZZ

Trevie reached up to touch the off-pink words floating in the air about him, amazed at the vibrant hues and the way they hung there unsupported by anything but their own weightlessness. Just before his finger touched them there was a *pop!* sound and he blanched. Turned his head around and searched, but saw nothing which could have made the noise. Nothing except the slowly encroaching shadows which didn't fade when he stared at them. They crept and accumulated until they formed a shape, a falseness he could finally dismiss. They developed a menace which all his foreknowledge could not then dispel.

He looked up again, more words flashed across the air before him.

BZZZZZZ!

This is your dream?

Stay in school!

Got Milk?

The little question mark after "milk" actually had a cute little eye embedded within and it winked at Trevie. Laughing, Trevie reached for the eye only to have it dissipate like the words before, followed by another sound, this one alarmingly loud. Insistent. Like a banging or violent buzzing.

Trevie tried to focus on the shadow people—to use them to push away the banging—it was just his mind playing tricks on him. Thinking he could only defeat those tricks with other, stronger tricks. The banging stopped. The buzzing did not. Trevie exhaled happily, feeling content and relieved.

"In. con. trol," he said to himself, but also to the bong. As if angered by his assurance, the banging came back a hundred times louder, a thousand times more emphatic. Sound reverberated through the room like an expanding tap-tom-tap echo, some Middle-Earth Moria shit. Until Trevie cupped his ears in his hands and curled up on the sofa, determined to lay still, wait the freaking shit out. Lying on his side he saw a cellphone lying in the recess under the coffee table's glass top. The thing was lighting up and vibrating against the metal sides of the recess. Reaching out a wavering hand, Trevie grabbed the device, wondering:

when did I put my cell there...

no wonder I lost it.

What a stupid place to put it.

Looking at the caller ID, Trevie read in jittery, pixelated letters: Alex Richardson. Fumbling and nearly dropping the phone, Trevie answered the call.

"Yo," he said, not hearing his own voice as it came out, croaked and strained, like a pleading whimper.

BZZZZZZ!

BZZZZZZZZZ!

Clarkless

Union Square, Manhattan, New York City.

"To weigh heavily on the mind."

"Go, TITTIES!" Clarkless screamed. The people around him gave him the stink eye. Even in the temperate darkness which surrounded them he could see their irises twinkle with annoyance and disdain. Nothing new. He was sitting amid a crowd of people in a medium sized theater, somewhere near Union Square. He had lost his phone somewhere, not sure when or where. No one had answered it any of the hundred or so times he or 2Day had called. Clarkless didn't want to have the thing disconnected because then he would have to call his Mom, have her get another one sent to him and activated and—

who the fuck knows how long the stupid bitch will take to do that?

Clarkless's thoughts came back into focus with a loud crash of sound from the stage in front of him. It was the sound of twenty or so heavy-soled feet pounding in unison. His head whipped up. There was 2Day wearing some god awful outfit, just like all the others on the stage. This dance was what she had been practicing for, for like, *weeks*. Apparently a third of her semester's grade depended on this fucking performance.

What a crock of shit school...

As 2Day started moving—her moves copied by the others around her—Clarkless heard 2Day's voice in his head screaming, "Step! Ball change! Step! Ball change! Turn! Turn! TURN!" He laughed a chittering, snort-like sound. Leaning against the back of his seat, he was suddenly tired, worn thin, aware he had not slept for several days. It was the longest he had stayed awake since the last time he binged with Alex Richardson. Thinking of Alex made him sigh. He would never admit it to 2Day (or to anyone else) but Clarkless wished that by some magic—had in fact planned his dreams of New York City around the possibility that he might run into Alex here. Have Alex see the new, brave, and dynamic person Clarkless had become. See that Clarkless had kept the name Alex had given him. See his genius in the making and be so compelled by it they ended up together again.

It was stupid and Clarkless knew it. But then what dream isn't inherently stupid on some level? Ignoring the stupidity of a dream and pressing further towards it, that was what eventually made a dream real. Though it never made a dream any less stupid. Clarkless yawned wide again, covering his mouth with a balled fist.

2Day danced furiously, doing quite well. Shockingly, she seemed to have remembered all the steps and gotten them right, yet to trip over herself or anyone else. They had agreed that she would be the one to smoke up the last of the stuff Trevie had gifted them. She needed to be awake, alert and energized. Clarkless hadn't bothered arguing. He was ready to come down, finding the idea of being consumed by tina repulsive.

At times it had seemed to Clarkless like Alex had been that way. Enslaved to the drug. 2Day seemed to be becoming the same. It wasn't that Clarkless didn't enjoy tina, just that somehow, intuitively, he knew that in order to achieve anything, he had to be able to ration himself. Ration his highs, harness them; not let them hang around him like a misty fog which some day would burn off when exposed to daylight, Leaving Clarkless naked and wasted, useless.

Who will want me then?

Another wave of foot-pounding crashed over him from the stage; the crowd around him cheered as dancers bowed and filed off the stage. Clarkless noticed most of the people around him were older, paired off.

Great. Parents everywhere.

He rolled his eyes. Rather than sitting back down from the standing ovation, he inched all the way down the aisle, oblivious of the people he stepped on, brushed against, or simply pissed off. At the end of the row, not bothering to look back, he turned and darted from the theater, made his way outside to the stage door where 2Day had said she would exit after the performance.

Minutes ticked by though he had little way of telling exactly how many. He refused to wear a watch, relying on his iPod or cell phone for the time. Watches were cheesy. The wait was interminable without some kind of guide as to how long it was taking, until the door burst open and 2Day came rushing out. All laughs and giggles. Unfortunately, following right on her heels was the dreaded Amber.

For a time Clarkless gaped at Amber.

Didn't we just have this conversation earlier today?

Sitting on a narrow twin bed in his room in Brooklyn, he and 2Day had both agreed to finally stop talking to Amber, to let her *fade away.*

We tweaked nipples on it!

Sighing, Clarkless glared at 2Day. She glared right back.

"*Lovely* dancing there, *Miss* Titties," Clarkless grumbled, bowing with feigned grace at 2Day. He did an impromptu skitter across the sidewalk, badly imitating the dancing the two girls had just done. 2Day laughed. Amber did not, only reinforcing to Clarkless that she did not belong with them.

But whatever.

"Thank you, faggot-sir," 2Day said with a flourish.

Amber smiled.

"You looked like an ogre in tap shoes, Amber," Clarkless said, flippantly waving at her.

If she has to be around I'm not gonna indulge her anymore.

2Day covered a giggle with her hand. Amber huffed, crossed her arms over her fat boobs and turned pointedly to 2Day.

"What*ever*. I'm going back to the dorm, are you coming?" Amber asked.

"Nah, I'm gonna hang with Clarkless," 2Day said, still snickering, "but maybe I'll see you later."

Flush with unexpected success, Clarkless smiled meanly in Amber's direction. The girl huffed, walked away, arms still crossed over her boobs.

"That was so mean," 2Day murmured as they walked into Union Square, punching him gently on the upper arm. Clarkless shrugged.

"So, what are we going to do? Has anyone called you about my phone?" Clarkless asked.

2Day grimaced. "Nopes! I was thinking we should..." But she stopped, voice trailing off. Her head swiveled, following someone. Clarkless tried to see what she was looking at. Though it was fairly dark, the streets were well lit and they were deep enough into Union Square now to be able to see fairly well.

"What are you looking...?" Clarkless asked, when he saw *exactly* what she was looking at.

A middle aged white guy with a large mustache. An unmistakable mustache. He was wearing a feathered blond wig, a blowsy shirt, and a pair of mom jeans. All of it hung over a pair of the biggest, clunkiest, non-stripper Wal-Mart heels Clarkless had ever seen. An equally aged woman, her brown hair loose and slightly wind-tussled, stood next to the man with the mustache, their hands intertwined.

"That. Is. Mr. Richardson," Clarkless breathed, hardly believing the words were true—could possibly *be* true—even as they came out of his mouth.

"I was just going to say the same thing," 2Day mumbled, shaking her head as though trying to dispel a hallucination.

"But, I mean, it *can't* be!"

"He's wearing a fucking wig! And mom jeans! And *heels.*

He's in fucking drag!" Clarkless exclaimed loudly, cutting off on the last words, suddenly afraid of being overheard by Mr. Richardson, who was now quite near.

"Should we go talk..." 2Day asked, but Clarkless pulled her away, out of the Square, back towards the theater from which they had come.

"No! What if it's *not* him? That would be so embarrassing! Is that even a real woman with him? It wasn't Miss Cathy! So not only is he in drag but he's *cheating* on Miss Cathy. Wow. No wonder Alex is so fucked up."

2Day leveled a steady, determined look at Clarkless. He knew that look. It was her infrequent "truth you need to hear" look. "Alex *wasn't* fucked up. You always said so. You just say that now because he dumped you."

Clarkless eyed her back, fierce. "Yeah well, maybe I changed my mind. I dunno. Fucking weird. I mean, part of me *really* wants to go talk to Mr. Richardson. That *has* to be him, we'll never see another guy with a mustache like that! I wonder if Alex knows. I know he and his dad didn't get along, but he would have said something if he knew his fucking dad was a *drag queen*." Clarkless sighed.

The sight—strange and exciting—of Mr. Richardson had pushed away most of Clarkless's tiredness. He was invigorated. Thoughts of Alex tumbled through his mind.

I'll search online later. See if I can at least figure out where Alex is now. Maybe he still has a blog somewhere.

"You're thinking about Alex again, you donkey-raping shit-eater," 2Day shouted, using one of their favorite South Park

163

references.

"I have not, nor will I *ever* rape an unwilling donkey, Miss Titties," Clarkless said, assuming a false air of aristocratic humor.

2Day laughed.

"So what now?" she said.

"I'm thinking about Alex," Clarkless confessed. She frowned.

"But *why*?" 2Day asked. "Just because we saw someone who looked like his fucking dad? I hardly remember the guy except for the mustache and the shitty attitude, we aren't even sure it was him, right?"

Clarkless shook his head, a little sad, a little annoyed. "It was him."

Without warning, his whole body sank in on itself. He was tired again; sluggish, with an urgent need to lie down somewhere. "Ugh. I think I'm going to go back to my place. I need some sleep. I've been awake too long."

"Do you think we like, *imagined* Mr. Richardson, maybe? Like we're so in sync we have the same freaky hallucinations? Somehow *feed* them to each other?" 2Day said, laughing.

Clarkless brushed her off with a wave. "Maybe. At this point, who knows? So you gonna be OK getting back to your place?"

She shrugged. "I don't wanna go home. Amber will be there. I'm not gonna want to be around her for a while, I think." She was looked back towards Union Square, bit her lip.

"Wondermus," Clarkless said. "I guess I'll see you

tomorrow, Tittymonster. Hopefully, I'll find my phone by then." He leaned over and hugged her, squeezed her boob. She reached up and tickled his under-arm, making him squeak.

"Ugh, I hate that!" he said. She wriggled her fingers at him and skipped off towards Union Square. Clarkless sighed, looked around in the dim light of the side street, wondered why he couldn't shake thoughts of Alex Richardson. Even seeing the man who looked like Alex's father—it wasn't Mr. Richardson, it couldn't be—it was more likely that because he had been thinking about Alex lately that he had found some way to connect the dots and see something which seemed related. That made more sense than whatever that weird apparition in the Square was.

No self-respecting drag queen would appear in public, in New York City, dressed so horribly anyway. Not unless the intent was to be funny or ironic, and there was nothing funny or ironic happening in those shoes. Those two had seemed very much like a couple of old people out on a *date*. Another reason to discount that it was Mr. Richardson. Clarkless moved on down the street towards the vague direction of the subway stop he needed. He could have gone towards Union Square and caught the train there, but something held him back. Part of it was not wanting to see that weird Mr. Richardson-ish thing again.

He was lost in thought, wondering where he had left his phone, and he nearly walked headlong into someone. Clarkless stepped back from the crash.

"Davis?"

Pritchard

East Flatbush, Brooklyn, New York City.

"To assemble closely and in large numbers, crowd."

Pritchard Mayer sped up. He wasn't exactly nervous around the variegated crowd of black people outside dear Trevor's apartment. But still, a certain *-ness* tickled him gently between the shoulder blades, a vague warning, a spider-sense. Pritchard took calming breaths, reminding himself of how close the subway stop was—only two more blocks. *I've fucked hundreds of black men. It isn't racist to be a bit frightened when surrounded by strangers, especially if they're all black, if they happen to be all black. What's the use of electing a black President if you still have to think in such terms?*

Pritchard sighed between gritted teeth, having forgotten to take calming breaths. Instead he walked faster—weaving between colorfully dressed yet still shabby people who seemed to pay him no mind. But that could be a ruse.

Think about something else.

After all, hadn't he been here numerous times without incident? Through still-gritted teeth, Pritchard finally took another calming breath. He had a mission.

One more block to go.

Casting around for something to take his mind off his surroundings, Pritchard called up the recent image of Trevor —*dear Trevor*—curled up in a fetal position on his couch, having buzzed Pritchard in. He would have opened the front door and gone right back to the couch. The man had been stark naked, his impressive cock forlorn, and strangely uninteresting. Pritchard had had sex with Trevor before. It had been mediocre; had the man not had such a huge dick it would have likely been eminently forgettable. But he had never seen the dealer so *out of sorts*. It was confusing and probably responsible for the feeling of being made supremely uncomfortable by the crowd surging around him. It happened sometimes. One image could seem to Pritchard to be an omen and from there everything would be shaped by that omen.

Still, Trevor *had* been lucid for the most part. They had talked while Pritchard weighed out half a pound of Trevor's tina. They smoked a bowl out of Trevor's water bong and Trevor did something odder still than the waiting-on-the-couch fetal position.

"Have you ever seen anything like this?" Trevor said as he held up a smartphone with a movie clip on it. Pritchard took the phone and played the clip. It was a young man, bound and gagged, a fuzzy object the size of a bowling pin being pushed in and out of the man's asshole. The video was obviously amateur work, and grainy besides, but the face of the person inserting the object was clear enough.

"As a matter of fact, dear Trevor, I have," Pritchard said, laughing. More, he recognized the face. A regular customer even. "Where did you get this phone?"

"Some faggot left it here. He was with a girl I was, maybe still am, you know, *doing*. Someone called and I answered, but they hung up and so I started looking around the phone, then *that* clip showed up. Crazy, right?" Trevor was trying to build up to something. Pritchard could feel it.

"Does it turn you on, Trevor?" Pritchard mumbled in a faux-deep voice. Trevor's eyes went wide and he looked well and truly frightened. "Nothing is going up my ass except tongues, Pritchie-Dick. Sorry. No, it's just, that face. It's familiar and I can't place it." Trevor scratched his head idly.

Pritchard shrugged and smiled blandly in return. He could put a name to the face for Trevor and Trevor would likely recognize it. The man behind that face was mildly famous, after all. But Pritchard was more discreet than that.

Shaking himself hard, Trevor eyed Pritchard, still nervous. "Can you take this phone, P? And get it back to whoever it belongs to? I dunno why but I just want it gone."

That's how it happened.

Pritchard sighed, but he eventually agreed. And now he was at the subway station, walking down concrete steps, little groups of *blacks* all around, but thankfully the sound of an upcoming train greeted him right away, along with the fetid stench of tunnel air. He looked at his watch. It was almost eight in the evening. He *should* be able to get home quickly enough, take care of whatever calls were necessary to handle returning the phone, and then be about his business for the rest of the evening. The train pulled in and Pritchard leapt aboard.

An hour later he was walking into the front door of his apartment. The familiar feeling of peace washed over Pritchard the instant he passed through the door. He supposed living in the same small space—a moderately sized studio apartment—for twenty years would have that affect on anyone. Whatever the magic of the place was, it insulated him from everything in such an effective manner he always felt a moment of purest peace at coming through that door.

Putting his bag down he took off his shirt, sat in his computer chair, his leather pants squeaking. He pulled his purchase from Trevor out of his messenger bag, along with the abandoned smartphone. Rather than search through the phone first for confirmation as to whom it might belong, he called his own phone to see if it came up.

It did not.

Then the abandoned phone rang.

Pritchard stared at it for a moment, recognized the name emblazoned on the abandoned smartphone the same way he recognized the face in the video before—they belonged to each other. Pritchard answered the call.

"Alex?" Pritchard said. "It's Pritchard."

Silence and breathing. "Pritchard? I... did I misdial?"

"I don't think so. It's a long story, but I recently came into possession of this phone and I do not know the owner, I had hoped when I saw your name and number on the caller ID that *you* might."

"I do. Clark. Clark Rhondes," Alex said. Something was off

in his voice. Pritchard heard it clear, but it was not easy to tell exactly what the cause might be. Since the commercial success of his last pseudo-confessional book, Alex Richardson had gotten a bit lost in drugs and sex. Such that Pritchard, at times, could not make much sense of the man nor the things he said. There were frequent, nonsensical calls. Paranoia. The usual meth-ish downfalls. Pritchard was used to those. But this was different. Alex sounded troubled, more than just fucked up.

"Well, have you any suggestions on how I might return this phone to said Mr. Rhondes?" Pritchard asked, suddenly eager to be done with the whole thing and off the phone with Alex. Whatever problems Alex was having, Pritchard wanted nothing to do with them. Alex was a good customer and an occasionally decent lay, but he was unbalanced in a way Pritchard found disconcerting.

People at times wondered openly to Pritchard: how had he existed as he had for so long? Continuously high on tina, frequently having gratuitous, anonymous orgy encounters—while keeping himself focused enough to work, sleep, learn, and grow. In short, how did he manage to avoid being consumed by the drugs and the attendant addictions of constant use? Pritchard knew it was balance which kept him even. He knew it without any inherent irony. But that was like knowing water was wet. How could he explain something he hardly understood himself?

Still, he sensed something off-kilter in Alex, enough out of whack that too much proximity might disrupt Pritchard's own balance. He was not sure if that was truly the case, but it felt like a deep truth and Pritchard believed in trusting his gut.

"I could come pick it up, I was looking to re-up anyway," Alex said, his voice doing that rare thing where you could hear his Southern accent. Normally so undetectable, it sometimes came through in a word here, a word there.

Pritchard reflected for a moment. He needed to make the sale, to make up for sales he had missed out on during the past week. And Alex was a good customer, always paying top prices, without discount even for large amounts. Pritchard could make his rent payment on this one transaction. And be rid of the phone.

"Well, that sounds... lovely. How soon can you be here?" Pritchard said, hoping his voice sounded sincerely warm.

"Thirty. I'm already dressed and ready," Alex replied

"Great. I'll see you shortly."

"See ya." The phone went dead. Pritchard set the phone aside and filled a bowl with a small amount of tina. Another fact of life by which he had learned to live.

Never over-smoke.

But then that too required balance. He sighed. After he smoked the bowl, Pritchard dug out his own phone and plugged it in to charge, noticing he had missed a call. Another regular customer—this one far more centered, as he, according to his own word, did not actually use the tina he purchased, using it only for guests and tricks.

Pritchard pressed the green dial icon.

"Davis here," came the reply.

"Davis. Pritchard. I saw you called?" Pritchard asked.

"Yes. I was hoping to stop by," Davis said, using his standard phrase indicating he wished to make a purchase. Pritchard knew Davis lived close by—closer than Alex, who was at least thirty minutes away and habitually ten minutes late. He could have Davis in and out before Alex showed up from his Upper West Side brownstone. Besides, that way he could hopefully resist getting caught up in anything with Davis. The man was *stunning* and a filthy-minded pervert of the first order, a combination Pritchard found irresistible when set with someone who did not use tina. Sex with Davis was *always* fun, *always* kinky and *always* long-lasting. This way Pritchard could resist the temptation, something he was not sure he could do otherwise.

"That would be fine. But soon," Pritchard said.

"I'm like four blocks away. I have someone with me though, I hope that's not a problem..."

Pritchard grimaced into the phone. It actually was a problem. He was certain Davis knew that very well. Unexpected, unknown guests did not and never would sit well with Pritchard—they led to prison. If he was with Davis, Pritchard could be relatively sure it was just a crackhead Davis had picked up off the street, gotten high with, and stupidly brought along. Pritchard deliberated and eventually decided he needed the money, paranoia be damned.

And maybe the trick is hot, too... those street punks sometimes are...

"Not a problem, Davis. As long as he's discreet." There was

173

no question it was a he. Pritchard knew Davis had a fag-hag—
a very close hag—but other than that he seemed to hate
women.

"Good. We'll be there soon."
Pritchard put his phone down next to the phone Trevor had
forced upon him. He smoked another small bowl and walked
around his apartment, making sure the place was in order. He
pulled out two chairs from a little recess so that the two guests
did not feel compelled to sit on his bed. That always seemed
to lead to more. Pritchard filled a medium-sized plastic baggie
with half an ounce of tina.

Minutes later there was a buzz on the door. Pritchard
buzzed the downstairs front door and unlocked the bolt on
his apartment door. He heard the steps as the men came up.
When the footfalls were near, he cracked his door and moved
back to sit in his computer chair to wait.

He heard the door creak open, more footsteps. "Pritch?"
came Davis's voice.

"Back here," Pritch called out, setting out the medium
baggie filled with tina next to the two phones on the desk.
Davis walked in wearing tight jeans and a dark blue t-shirt—
loose fitting, but his lean musculature showed through. The
guy behind Davis caught Pritchard's eye. Pritchard shifted his
cock in his leather pants without thinking. The guy was
young. Not as young as Anton, but close. He was prettier, too,
but in a masculine way, not at all androgynous and soft like
Anton. Well, Anton was not soft, precisely—at least not
physically—but something of his *inner* softness came through

to Pritchard when he looked at the kid. Not this kid, though. He was tall, lanky, with an oval shaped face and large chin, a slight dimple in the center of it. His hair was a dusty brown and cut so he had a small sweep of bangs across his forehead. His skin was a little bad—apparent acne scars, blackheads on his nose—but the effect was not unattractive. Something about the guy was familiar.

"Pritch, this is Clarkless," Pritchard heard Davis say, but he had already extended his hand to the guy.

He might look masculine, but his hands are soft and he sways like a fag. Still, that's kind of hot, too.

The young man, Clarkless, shook Pritchard's hand vigorously, maybe a little too much so. He smiled widely as well—was he flirting? Pritchard didn't have a patch on Davis for looks. He was more than twenty years older, his body fading from its muscular past, still nice and shapely, but saggy in places, no longer as tight and taut as it once was. Still, it was always more than enough to get him what he desired.

"Fantastic to meet you, Clarkless. What an interesting name," Pritchard said. All his thoughts of avoiding any entanglement between Alex and Davis had fled. Clarkless blushed a bit and looked sheepishly at Pritchard. Davis grinned a little.

Like a key turning in a lock Pritchard knew how the young man was familiar.

That face. That bowling pin. And Alex Richardson. How is this possible in a city as big as New York?

"I gave it to myself when I moved to New York. I wanted

175

to leave everything else behind," Clarkless said.

Davis snickered. "I knew him when he was still *Clark*."

Pritchard's head tilted towards the phones on the computer desk behind him as he pictured this Clarkless as "Clark Rhondes" having a bowling pin slammed into his rectum and crying out with pleasure. The other two followed Pritchard's gaze.

"That's... that looks like my phone... I lost it yesterday," Clarkless mumbled.

"Clark Rhondes?" Pritchard asked. He could tell by the shock on both their faces he was right.

"Um. Yeah?" Clarkless said. "How did you know, where did...?"

Davis elbowed Clarkless. Pritchard smiled at them, his mind stuck on that video, ever so pleased that this pretty young man was a kinky pig as well.

I should have known. He's with Davis after all...

He grabbed the phone, intending to hand it back to its owner. The young man obviously wanted to know where Pritchard found the phone. Telling him would mean revealing Pritchard's connection to Trevie, something which Pritchard had never allowed himself to do. Would not do so now, even though it was clear that Clarkless also knew Trevie.

Small fucking world!

"The phone was given to me," Pritchard said, making a mental note to contact Trevie and let him know to keep the cat in the bag, "by an acquaintance who asked me to track its owner down." Pritchard remembered Alex and, as if the memory were a summons, the front buzzer went off. Pritchard could not keep the look of indecision and shock off his face. Davis and Clarkless turned to look at one another, then back at him.

"Is everything, OK...?" Davis asked, looking towards the hallway leading to the door. Pritchard nodded, distracted. He was at a loss now. *What to do? What to say? What not to say? How to explain?* It was Alex Richardson downstairs, and that meant he would not be able to indulge this Clarkless. *No bowling for me!* Worse, the size of his apartment and the building meant there was no way to keep the visitors from running into each other. The buzzer rang insistently. Alex would not go away; it was not in his constitution.

Pritchard sighed.

"I have someone else coming over, and he's early. To be frank," Pritchard cringed inwardly, feeling sure this was going to come back to bite him, as he spoke to Clarkless. "I think he knows *you*, young man. In fact, I was going to release your phone into his custody, as he had called it earlier. Strange as it is, I answered and discovered he was already known to me, so I agreed to let him return it to you."

"You answered my phone?" Clarkless said, his eyes wide with the mystery of it all, "Um, who is he?"

Pritchard bit his lower lip. It went against every part of his nature to mix his customers up in this manner. It could so easily get him dragged into something which could end very badly. But as they already knew each other...

"His name is Alex."

Both of his visitor's faces went East German with shock.

Jules

8ᵗʰ Avenue, Chelsea, New York City

"To force into service."

Jules waltzed back into her living room. Prather sat calmly on her futon. He looked with interest at the photos on the walls, side tables, and atop the entertainment center. She leaned over and set his drink on the coffee table. It was just a glass of ice water, but she had put it in her nicest, non-plastic glass. She sidled in next to him and sipped at her Red Bull and vodka.

As she opened her mouth to say something, Prather did the same. A flush rose into her cheeks. She looked away for a half-second then turned back to him, flipping her hair as she did so. A small, impish smile spread across her face. Inside her a determination set in to let Prather speak first. *It doesn't destroy feminism to let a man speak first.*

"You were about to say..." Jules said.

He wasn't smiling.

Is that a good sign or a bad one?

Smiling was not something Prather did offhand—Jules had figured that out about him already—so maybe it was neither. Her nerves were getting the best of her and she forced herself to think of nothing, but that never worked. It didn't work now. Prather finally nodded. She expected some argument—some lighthearted comment where he told her to speak first. Urged her to do so, requiring her to respond in kind—but that never came.

Instead Prather said: "There is something happening between us, Jules. I am not sure if you have felt it." She could only stare moon-faced.

Is he serious?

Of course he is. He always is, even when he's being funny.

A flash of insight struck her: *maybe that's what it takes to be a truly successful and liberated artist, a genuine creatively inspired person, an actualized creator. Maybe?*

You not only needed that Muse of the Moment, but you had to be *serious* about it—*always*—even when it seemed you were not.

Maybe that's why rock stars and poets always become addicts, because they take their pleasures as seriously as their art?

Jules made a pleased humming noise as the thoughts tumbled through her. Prather arched an eyebrow and she blushed further in response.

"You are thinking something. What is it?" Prather said. At first she wanted to reply with sarcasm. Like her second nature required it, but she swallowed that thought. Because there was no way he had meant it *that* way—could never have meant it *that* way. He would never say something so stupid; of course she was thinking something, people were *always* thinking something. But could she tell him what she was truly thinking?

Yes. I can.

180

She swallowed hard and told him what she had been thinking. If this was going to be the *real* thing, the *"one,"* then it had to be different. All her evasions had to fall away

Or what's the point?

Prather looked to be carefully considering her words. She leaned back into the sofa and a little bit away from him. Some things she couldn't control and she was nervous.

Would he scoff at her insight?

"I am not sure I take *every*thing seriously, Jules. But when a person commits their life to something, when the two are one and the same, the seriousness is implicit, and it if is not, then you are either the luckiest person alive or the least." She furrowed her brow, tried work out what that meant.

Inexplicably, no warning given, no underlying reason supplied, he smiled wide and bright as though some inimitable truth had just occurred to him. She smiled back without pausing to think.

"You have such a beautiful smile," Jules murmured. It was true. He stopped smiling—but slowly, languidly.

"I don't think we should see each other again after tonight, Jules," Prather said, as if it were a compliment, a banal comment, a piece of *common sense* advice.

The price of milk.

Jules blinked, unsure she had heard what she thought she had heard.

Didn't he just... aren't we going to... isn't he...?

She sunk into herself, like her skin was the fabric of a hot air balloon and the burner had been rudely turned off. The fire quenched, the billowing folds of colorful fabric still flowing but ever closer to collapsing, the deflation impossible to stop. His arm was still around her, but suddenly it felt hard and unwelcoming, still hot but not at all warm.

"But... I... I..." she mumbled. He made no move to stop her —no move to forestall—did nothing but stare. His wide brown eyes so expressive, so open—so apparently understanding—so at odds with his words. So completely distant, unreachable.

Jules' jaw snapped shut and made a loud click, jarring her teeth. Before she could even make a mental move to block them from coming, tears welled.

Great. I'm going to be THAT girl. Again. And again. And again.

Still he stared, his arm holding her down in place, keeping her from falling between the cushions into the sofa, forgotten and deflated.

"Jules..." Prather started, and though he paused, there was no catch, no uncertainty, no insecurity. Like the pause was just for her, to show her he, too, could be in doubt, or at least understand lesser people could be. Superman feigning the effects of icy weather on exposed skin. She looked away, knowing she should get up, make him leave. Spare herself this and the next moment, but she couldn't. It was perverse, felt entirely wrong, but she knew it would happen. Knew that there was little enough strength in her at that moment to cajole her to stand up, make him leave. For now, maybe forever, he would rule part of her and she knew it. Maybe he

182

knew it as well.

"It is not what you think, Jules. I have never..." Prather paused and this time it was *real*. Superman's perfectly sculpted chest beneath her soft touch. His expression confirmed it, as if he had never known such realness, such doubt within himself. Confronted by it then, did not know how to react, how to express what he felt, he lacked the language. *I bet he could fucking paint it though.* Prather swallowed hard and *he* looked away. Jules stopped slouching into the sofa. Her neck straightened and she wiped her eyes, never letting them leave Prather. *He* looked away. An emotional abyss yawned beneath her, huge and terrifying, an edge alongside blackness which roared with silent need. Yet she wasn't alone, wasn't facing it with only a half-assed best-friend yelling from inside the chasm, that the fall was quite pleasant *once you got used to the wind against your face*. Something inside her snapped, altered, transformed. For the first time ever, Jules was unfettered, freed. She smiled, a smile so wide it made her cheeks hurt.

Like the Bad Seed.

Prather turned back to face her and caught sight of her smile. He now looked uncertain and off-balance. She had thought him so strong, so secure, so confident. And here he was before her, revealed: unsure, weakened, and for some reason—some inexplicably grand, unfathomable reason—*insecure*.

Had she just thought he would rule her? She wanted to laugh.

"Jules. You see something in me. I see it every time you look at me, and I cannot live up to that. You deride me with compliments, and then you profess deep affection for me in subtle comments and introductions. There is no more to me than my art, Jules. It's my *life*. Everything else is just need and satisfaction. That is not something you can offer someone else, not something which can be cherished in building a life together. Though I am not sure what it is, there's something between us. It does *not* mean I can give you what you need."

Jules blinked rapidly at him.

What else do I need?

His presumption caught her off guard, quite beside the fact that not so deep down she *knew*: he was right. She did need something and though she had seen that something in him, he was refusing to share it. Refusing to even admit it existed. Could she fault him for that?

I can.

I will.

The something which had changed within her grew, an elixir of determination spreading outward through her circulatory system.

"You're afraid, Prather. I expected more," Jules said, surprised by the hardness in her voice, the firmness of her tone, the strength of will leaking out of her words and into her spine, making her sit up straight and level a gaze firmly at him. There were no more tears forthcoming. Not this time. For his part, Prather blinked and looked down at his lap, a pose of defeat. He pulled his arm from around her and it was like the

184

last shot fired in a horrible civil war. The very last soldier wobbling, unsure if a bullet had pierced the skin—or was it the sudden, quiet boom of a peaceful ending? The certain knowledge it had never been Prather's war; he had been pressed unwilling, and now it was over. Jules saw all that in the motion of Prather's arm as it left her.

"I'm afraid," Prather said, not making eye contact. "And you deserve better than my fear." Prather made to stand up, the indication he would leave written all over his face, in the language of his lithe body. Jules took a deep breath, the scent of him rushing into her and she breathed it in, knowing it would be the last time, the last scent, the strongest memory she would retain of him. She clenched her jaw, unwilling to let herself say any of the things flashing in her mind, none of the pleading she had done with the Bad Seed, nor any of the arguing she had done with Davis, nor any of the cajoling she had done with her family. The needling and loud-capping which had eventually become too much, separating her from all her siblings and finally her parents, forcing her family to walk around her as if on glass, on eggshells. Masterfully, she held all that back. Managed to keep her eyes tight on Prather. Not quite a glare, but not a carefree glance either.

"I should go," Prather said. She heard the word "should" louder than the others. It had a special ring to it, a truth of the doubt within him. It was a humanizing word. Jules' jaw quivered with the effort of holding it closed. Operated by something else, the new something which had blossomed from deep within her, she responded.

"No. You shouldn't. You *should* stay."

He blinked at her. Stunned. Confused. Words came to her, words she hadn't known were inside of her. Words imbued with both the confidence and precision Jules had felt in *him*. The qualities she had been sure would never be hers, and therefore the most attractive to her. She imagined herself speaking not just to him, but to all the men who had left her dry over the years. The words spilled out.

"You said it yourself. You feel something between us, and even as frightened as you are, you don't deny it. It won't go away. Maybe you'll paint about it, some extravagantly beautiful thing that inspires and bewilders everyone who sees it. But not you, because you'll know it's just a shadow of *me*. A shadow of what you feel—no, felt! Of what you were too *chickenshit* to chance! A shadow of the art you *could've* made had you been willing to try something you weren't sure you could do. Isn't that what you've *always* done? Huh? Brilliant, amazingly talented Prather! Going through the motions. The need and satisfaction and the painting! All of it! Just routine! Just killing time! None of it taking a chance at failure. And none of it coming close to succeeding at truly making you *lastingly* happy. Just ointment over a persistent rash."

When words finally failed, she choked up, started to angry-cry. Jules took deep breaths to calm herself. It was like she had been a sudden Pod Person. She had spoken words carved out of her own heart, though never words she herself could have, nor would have, spoken. A possession.

Prather stood. Loomed over her. Looking down at her,

arms at his side, fists balled and pressed against hips. There was no anger apparent. He just *stood*, staring down, pensive.

"You might be right," he said, "but I still should go."

Jules flew off the couch and pushed hard into him, shoved him double-handed towards the door. Despite being lithe and lean he was still solid and tall, but Jules had rage on her side. Prather stumbled backwards. "Leave then! Fucking GO! Just like everyone else! Just like fucking Davis, you FUCKERS. You are just like the Bad Seed, just like my family, just like everyone else! All any of you do is run, think of yourselves— never the damage you leave behind. Well *fine*. I can take it." She cried in earnest now. Drops of salted, determined anger. "I will be *fine*. Go. Fucking leave, asshole." Jules looked away, sobbed into her hands.

When she heard the door shut behind him, she fell onto the sofa face first. She let the wracking sobs shake her body until she slid from the sofa, fitfully, onto the floor. Her wet face pressed against the parquet flooring, the throw carpeting bunched beneath her. Still streaming tears leaked on the vinyl floor—the small ridges of the tiles pressed, forced themselves against her cheek. She was that fallen soldier now. The bullet passed cleanly through her.

Anton

8th Avenue, Chelsea, New York City

"To use in a manner other than intended."

Anton stood in front of the large, full body mirror covering half a wall in Sir's bathroom. The whole room was tiled in luminous black squares. Silver furnishings shimmered on the sink, towel racks, and even the hardware on the shower and garden tub. Sir was clearly wealthy—likely independently so —not having to work at all. Sir's Alex was also clearly a young trophy lover. Sir had not called him a husband or anything other than "Alex" yet. Even fucked up as he was, the name Alex rang all kinds of bells in Anton's mind. The wetness dripping down the back of his legs, the welts on his ass and back from the beatings; Anton still tasted all the filth he had swallowed, still smelled what he had rubbed all over his face amid the ecstasy. But looking in the mirror, he saw an apparition, a ghost. The real him, the living him, had burned off. Like cut in a bowl of molten meth. Wavering in front of that mirror was no longer Anton, but a *toy*, a piece of meat for the use of Sir. A tool to be used, a hole to be filled, a face to be degraded and humiliated—or cast aside should the toy no longer be of pleasure and value.

Anton's small dick vibrated in time with such thoughts. He had no foolish dreams Sir would keep him around permanently. Sir had used Anton hard, seemed to enjoy their playtime. And Anton reveled in that, felt rightness, as though he had met fate head on. Embraced it like a foundling Mother and found the solace which came along with such moments. The aligning of purpose when the universe around you rang with simple, unadulterated *correctness*. It was fleeting, and it took drugs and nasty sex to reach such an acme, but that was just part of the ugly grandeur of it all. *Nothing beautiful in life can be reached without seeing the ugly first! Maybe everything needs to be ugly before it can be considered beautiful...*

Alex, not Sir's Alex, but the first Alex—the one who had shaped Anton into the pleasure suck he now was—had said those words to Anton.

Not that Anton didn't entertain hopes and desires: hope these emotions could last, desire they might never fade. But he knew better—*he knew.* There was a correlation between who he was and what he needed. Hope and desire yearned for that humiliation, that rough use. The two were orbits which met up every million moments or so, crashing mightily when they did, forever altering the course of those bodies, changing everything. But never for a moment defeating the fact they continued to float through space, alone. Only total destruction would truly change anything.

He saw Sir moving behind him in the mirror. A smaller, less potent version of Sir, shrunken now that the abuse was stopped, paused. Or was it just a reflex of Anton's to lessen the blow of coming rejection by shrinking his desire's potency? Sir came no closer. Sir's Alex took over the reflection, growing large until Anton saw and felt the young man hovering behind him. His face was impassive, calm, as though he were steadying himself for something unpleasant yet making an effort not to appear so.

"Um. Anton?" Alex said."Can you..."

More emotions welled up inside Anton: rage, hurt and rejection. Was this always to be his destiny? Sweet humiliation chased with bitter rejection? To be used, to enjoy it so much more than anything else and then be thrown away after? Could there not be an exception? He knew the nature of being used precluded more, it was incompatible to want humiliation and expect it to flow from someone who *cared* for you.

Only a fag would want that. Or imagine it could exist at all.

And Anton craved that fantasy. Wanted to be loved and shat on by the same man. Beaten and coddled in consecutive motions, bound and thereby freed, forever, by the same man —or men.

By a man like Sir.

But here was the true object of Sir's affections, if not his humiliations. The reason Anton was there at all was because Sir loved this Alex and would not debase him. Would not abase Sir's own love by abusing his Alex, not as Anton had been used, *needed* to be used. To do so would cheapen Sir's love and clearly the man could not reconcile that.

These thoughts were new to Anton. They floated around the nebulous interior of his mind, sticking to nothing, unable to coalesce into a philosophy. They were like the shards of a kaleidoscope, shifting into something beautiful and then turning again before the beauty could be fully appreciated. He simply could not hold on to them, make them stay.

Alex must have seen the struggle on Anton's face because he recoiled. He looked back towards Sir and sighed before he faced Anton again. "Sir is, um, out of tina. He wonders if you could get more?"

Anton's rage drizzled away. *What?* He looked doe-eyed at Alex and smiled. His face was still filthy in places, his body sweaty and his teeth stained, yet still he smiled for all he was worth. His hope and desire were not mutually exclusive bodies meant to crash and continue on separately; maybe he *could* have it all. Be a part of something larger than himself. Maybe this was how it had to be. The love going to an *Alex*, the abuse going to an *Anton.* It could be complete for all of them. Anton licked his lips. His dick was rigid.

"Yeah, sure. Just need to make a call. How much does Sir want?" Anton asked.

Alex took a deep, relieved breath. Anton wondered whether Sir had sent Alex in here for this or if it was Alex's idea. It didn't really matter. Alex and Sir had both gotten high with Anton—nowhere near as high as Anton had gotten, but they had used more than expected. Not a new pleasure for Anton, but it seemed to be new for them. Alex smiled.

"Well, as much as you think we'll need for the next month or so," Alex said.

Anton went lighter than air. His heels rose gracefully from the ground, his ass poking backward with joyful need. "For all three of us?" he asked with hesitant excitement. Drawn up and full of beautiful, warm air—about to rise up-out of himself with sweetness, Anton batted his eyes. Alex nodded.

"Sir wants you fully trained."

Anton beamed, leaned back against the black tiles which covered the sink top. The moment was surreal—full and nearly overwhelming—as strong and addicting as any moment of humiliation and use had ever been, disconcerting while also fulfilling.

Is this for real?

"Are you and Sir... married?" Anton asked, unsure where the question came from, only knowing it had been floating around his mind. As happy as he was now, it had been freed.

Alex blinked. "Sir doesn't believe in marriage. I am his partner. You might become our slave. *If you can be properly trained.*"

Anton felt Sir's hovering presence just outside the door before the man himself entered. Alex deftly moved aside so Sir stood, leaned, over Anton. "You really want to be our slave, boy?" Sir asked, tone firm, implacable. But his eyes twinkled. The combination sent thrills through Anton unlike anything he had ever felt. He luxuriated in the feeling before replying.

"Yes, Sir!" There was not a moment's hesitation in the addition of "Sir" this time. Sir nodded, pleased. He held up a wad of crisply rolled hundred dollar bills. "Go get whatever supplies you need for the next month. Alex is going to go buy some new toys and a full-body latex suit for you. I expect you back here in three hours. Do you understand, slave?"

Anton nodded furiously, a child pleased with his role as a

child to a father even more pleased with his role as a father.

Anton set the money on the counter and took a quick, pointless shower, gargled with hot water and spit the brown results into the drain. He got dressed, pocketed the money, counting it as he did so. His hands shook at the amount. Was it a test of some kind? Sir had given him eight thousand dollars! Anton called Trevie's phone several times, but no one answered. That left Pritchard. Anton knew Pritch would never have even close to the necessary half-pound ready, but it would be a start. Anton could buy everything Pritchard had and then leave the rest to Trevie, maybe even get Pritchard to deliver it.

He made sure to explain all of this to Sir before leaving. Sir nodded and waved him off, Alex already dressed and gone. As he started for the door, Sir pulled Anton by the neck with one firm hand, drawing Anton close enough to smell Sir's ripe armpits. Sir whispered into his ear. "I've never used a boy like you before, slave. I want more. *Lots more.* Don't fuck me over." Sir released Anton's neck and Anton stared lovingly into Sir's coal-colored eyes.

How could he explain to Sir that he would never leave? That this was everything he wanted? That ever since the first time he had been used—used hard in a way he never expected, abused and debased until he found it fit—that it was what he had always been meant for, though he had not known it. How could he explain he would never want to leave? Any promise would sound as hollow coming from his mouth as it would entering Sir's ears. *All promises are hollow.*

press >franklet

Anton vaguely knew that truth, suspected Sir did also. What he could do was nod, his head bouncing up and down furiously until Sir waved him off. Outside Sir's building Anton nervously misdialed as he attempted to call Pritchard before he got it right. No answer. He called several more times then gave up and, half-running, made his way to the subway station undeterred. Once he reached the stop nearest Pritchard's in Chelsea he tried calling again as he exited the station, but still got no answer. He loped the next few blocks, the excitement of everything combining with the jones for more tina making him shake uncontrollably.

Part of him simply could not believe it was all happening. At Pritchard's building Anton rang apartment 2B. Pritchard seriously disapproved of unannounced visitors, but Anton was too jittered by the moment to care much. He had a need and the need *must* be met. Surprisingly, the front door mag-lock was buzzed open almost immediately. As though Anton had been expected, and Pritch was hovering near the button. Wasting no time contemplating what that quickness might imply, Anton flew up the stairs.

The door to 2B was open. A slight crack spewed light and sound from inside Pritch's apartment to the hallway. Anton paused—wary now—but need impelled him. He pushed the door open, went inside. No one was waiting near the door, but over the sound of low-volume porn Anton heard furtive voices, grunting. Pritchard did not have a large apartment: a simple studio with a bathroom near the front door, a long hallway of closet space leading to the main area which

194

contained a small kitchen and a large bedroom/living room. Anton made his way down the hallway towards the voices as his body shook. Much more than it had before the nervousness reached a vibrant and strange pitch, strange even for Anton. A portent of something feral and amazing. Anton reached up a shaking arm and stared at his hand, tried to focus, to tell his arm and hand to be still, but nothing worked —if anything, both shook harder.

"H-he-hello?" Anton asked, annoyed that his voice shook. The hallway emptied into the large studio space. There was Pritchard's computer desk next to the flat-screen TV, both situated in front of a rubber-sheeted bed, a few chairs placed alongside the bed. All of that was normal, expected even. But Anton caught sight of who was there, none of whom were expected. He could hardly breathe from the shock of what he saw. He became so fixated, his whole body went limp.

"Alex?" Anton murmured, eyebrows climbing up his damp forehead. "Davis?" Anton said next, hardly trusting his eyes at the sight of these two men together, here of all places. One a ghost from his old past, the other a zombie from his new. He saw they sat as far from each other as the self-contained room would allow. Between them was a boy, older than Anton but not by much, a year or two at most. He was not as pretty as Anton, nor as delicate, but he was thin, handsome, boyish, and attractive enough that Anton was immediately jealous of his presence in the room amongst *these* men. He could already feel his own light dimmed by the other boy, he wanted to growl. His allegiance to the dream Sir offered could only go so

195

far. Few things could prick Anton's ire like another faggot his age stealing his fire. Old men were safe in that regard. It was why Anton preferred older men. They did not operate with the same cold fission he did, their light was hot fusion. Though, really, none of these men were old, except maybe Pritch, whose age Anton could not guess with any certainty. Pritch looked at Anton with a well-shaped eyebrow arched, sensing that something existed between the gathered men. Pritch's raised eyebrow said he was not entirely sure what that something could be. *Or maybe that's just what I want to think.* He could not tell. Before Alex or Davis could reply to Anton, Pritchard—sitting in his large black captain's chair in front of his computer desk, crossed legs in leather chaps, a bemused expression on his face – spoke.

"Dear little Anton. You know how I feel about unannounced visitors..." Pritchard said, his words sounding like a scolding, though the tone spoke the opposite. It was lighthearted, bemused. "But seeing as we were all *just* talking about you, I suppose it fits that you've magically arrived." Pritchard barked a little, devilish laugh. He waved a small water bong at Anton.

"Wanna hit?"

Trevie

East Flatbush, Brooklyn, New York City

"Any manner of the devices used to apply pressure."

Bzzzzz.
How did a bee get in here?
Bzzzz.
Fuckin' bees. Hate 'em.

Trevie looked up from the piece of the floor upon which he had been focusing. His eyes darted around the room, looking for the damnable and insistent bee which was buzzing around.

Maybe I can do some Mr. Miyagi shit and squash the fucker if it comes close enough.

But the buzzing suddenly stopped, leaving Trevie to wonder, laconically, if bees existed. Or if perhaps it was just the shadow-people playing games with him, *again*.

Fuckin' shadow people. And bees. They're in this shit together, I know it.

His roving eyes landed on the coffee tabletop, where a plastic sack of tina shards lay next to his water-bong. Blinking at the bag, Trevie wondered when he had gotten it from the safe. He could not remember leaving the couch since he had spoken to Pritchard. As if summoned by the old queen's name, the bees started their buzzing again.

BZZZZZZ.

Only it was louder, angrier now.

What was angrier than a bee?

Trevie's mind reeled. The coffee-tabletop trembled and vibrated, like the hand of a man with Parkinson's.

How the hell can a bee do that?

Trevie's mind cleared like a fart in a hurricane, if only for a second.

It can't. A bee can't shake a coffee tabletop.

It just can't!

Magically, a phone appeared further down the table-top behind the bong and the sack of tina. It twittered across the glass of the tabletop, begging for attention. Trevie laughed — weak, relieved — and murmured:

"Fuckin' bees. Shit."

Trevie grabbed the phone, paused before answering, stared with longing at the bong. *I need a hit.* How long had it been? *Who fuckin' knows, yo.* He could barely make out the little boxy letters on the caller ID. Turning the device over in his hands, he wondered: *is it even my phone?* The shadow-people fluttered in non-committal response. Shrugging at the shadow-people, Trevie answered the call.

"Um. Yo?" he said, voice wavering.

"Trevor, dear! I am *ever so happy* you actually answered," a smarmy man said.

Trevie's mind worked like an adding machine, with a

mechanical tick clicking away until it recognized the voice, spit out a result. The voice, for its part, seemed to expect this, well aware of Trevie's idiosyncrasies and waiting appropriately.

"Pritch?" Trevie said, relieved. It must be his phone after all. Why would he think it was someone else's? Why did that tug at his memory?

"Yes, dear Trevor. I find that I am in rather dire need of your services."

Trevie blinked and looked over at the sack of tina, suddenly remembering how it had gotten there. Pritchard had stopped by hours before and helped Trevie get the sack out of the safe. Trevie's face went ashen as he recalled sitting on the couch, shouting out the combination numbers to Pritchard.

He could have stolen everything. FUUUUCK!

The shadow-people snarled a cold laughter at him.

Trevie waved a dismissive hand at them.

Trevie had not left the couch after all. Trevie's fingers itched to go and check, make sure all his money and drugs and shit was still there. Even as fucked up as he was, he found he trusted Pritch—still there *was* a limit. Which brought up a question, one he blurted out before it swarmed around his mind, overwhelmed everything else.

"How can you need more? You were just here," Trevie said. His mind clarified again, some normalcy returning. He felt the first rush of embarrassment and annoyance at how he had spent the past several days, hours, or whatever—however long it had been—frozen in stasis on the couch.

What did I take besides tina?

He couldn't remember, but he must have taken something.

How long have I been awake?

No clue. Bzz, a snarky voice in Trevie's mind replied

Pritch's voice pulled him back from his questions. "Yes, Trevor dear. Nearly fifteen hours ago." There was chiding in Pritch's voice, though it washed off Trevie before it could stick —which was normal for him. What did stick was the number fifteen. Trevie gaped at the sack of meth.

Fifteen hours? What the fuck?

Bzz.

"OK. Um. I guess you need it now. You comin' over?"

"Cannot do it, Trevor, dearheart. I rather need you to come here," Pritchard said. Trevie's insides tightened. Pritch had insisted on delivery only a few times before, rarely enough to warrant questions from Trevie every time. And always for amounts far larger than anything Pritch himself would ever deal. Trevie knew Pritch was deeply afraid of being busted, and thus would never allow himself to transport such large amounts. Still, something was off. Trevie sensed it, but he pushed that feeling away, thinking instead it must be some holdover of whatever had been consuming him on the couch during the past day or two.

Bzzzzz.

Fuckin' bees.

Bz.

"Um. OK then. How much?" Trevie asked.

"All of it," Pritch said. "A half."

That could mean a bunch of things. But Trevie remembered Pritch had seen the safe, which meant the man knew how much Trevie had left in stock for sale.

He can't know about the second stash.

Can he?

As Trevie considered this, he realized the request spoke to Pritch's honesty. If Pritch had taken more than the usual amount he purchased he likely would not be calling for more now. Trevie swallowed, hard. *It must be a half-pound then.* A half-pound was a lot of fucking tina. Pritch had never bought so much, nor tried to arrange for more than half that. Trevie licked his lips. Pritch did pay top dollar. This sale would set Trevie up for a month, maybe two. He could buy three or four pounds of stock, and, combined with what he had in the safe, maybe even manage to pay his rent after.

"Shit. Um. OK," Trevie said as he tried to organize his thoughts. "I'll be there in an hour."

"So quickly? Well, fantastic. We shall be here," Pritchard said. The phone went dead. Trevie's hand hung in midair as he stared at the phone like it was a live snake surrounded by angry killer bees.

Fuckin' bees.

We? Pritchard had said WE. What the fuck?

Bzzzzzz.

Trevie's hand shook with fear.

Was it a set up? It couldn't be. Not with Pritchard.

Still, once the thought was lodged in Trevie's mind he found no easy way to remove it. Until an easy way presented itself. What he needed was someone who knew both Pritchard and himself, someone they could trust. A name flashed behind his eyes...

Prather.

Grinning at his ingenuity, Trevie called the man. After four rings, Prather answered, "Trevie?"

"Yo! Prath-dog. I need a big, big fuckin' favor." It occurred to Trevie, sudden and striking, that Prather did not know Pritchard. It was Anton who knew Pritch. *Fuck me. Bzzz.* He swatted the air, distracted. *Why did I think of Prather then?* Memories of Prather asking him to search for Anton flooded Trevie's thoughts. Trevie's mind worked as fast as it could.

Bzzzzzzzzz.

"You still looking for little Anton?" Trevie asked, trying to mask any sneakiness in his voice.

"I guess I am?" Prather said. "Yes. I am. Have you found him?"

"Maybe. I need you to go visit a friend of mine named Pritchard. Anton was there recently and you can get him, I mean Pritchard, to um, help you track A down. I'm sure of it. Cool?"

Trevie waited, holding his breath for Prather to respond. Seconds drew past before the reply came. "Alright."

Trevie wanted to fist bump the air. Instead, he swatted at the phantom bees. The shadow-people clicked with amusement in the near distance.

"Fuckin' fantastic. OK, here's the address. So, I'm on my way over there now to make a delivery. I was hoping you'd meet me there, and maybe go up first and make sure everything is cool..."

Trevie bit his lip. As shady as it all must sound, Prather had already promised and Trevie knew he would stand by that word. Silence stretched.

"I suppose that is fine. Though I could wish you had said such first," Prather said.

Trevie grinned. "Yeah! Totally. Sorry. It's just. Well, you know how I do, Prath-dog. Here's the address." Trevie rattled off the address to Pritchard's apartment in Chelsea. "I'll be there in like forty-five to an hour? See you then?"

"I'll be waiting outside," Prather said. "Goodbye, Trevie."

Trevie hung up the call, gathered his messenger bag, pulled a half-pound of tina from the safe and stuffed it into the bag's hidden, sewn-in pocket. He washed his face, swished some mouthwash. On impulse he changed his clothes to a relatively clean set—black sneakers, a navy blue hoodie, baggy jeans, and a tight grey skullcap—thinking that might attract less unwanted attention. He threw the messenger bag over his left shoulder.

He was about to walk out the door when his eyes landed on the bong and he remembered he needed a hit before he left. Trevie removed the messenger bag and set it down, made his way over to the bong. With practiced skill he added a huge shard to the bowl and lit up. Pulling the cut off with a few quick inhalations, Trevie swirled the bowl around over the butane torch, angled the flame steady on the bottom of the bowl. He took a long, deep breath. Feeling flooded into him, his whole body nearly went slack with it. He almost dropped the bong in response, catching himself at the last moment, giggling, as the water inside sloshed with a disturbing similarity to the sound of bees buzzing.

BZZZZZZ. BZZZZZ!

"Heh. Fuckin' bees," Trevie muttered as he set the bong down, grabbed his bag, and rushed out the door.

Alex

8th Avenue, Chelsea, New York City

"To advance eagerly; push forward."

Alex Richardson looked around the room, making sure not to let his eyes linger too long upon any one face. It boggled the functioning part of his mind that he was sitting, calmly surrounded, by *these* people. One such weird confluence of chance he could easily accept. Two was stretching credulity. Three implied the Universe itself was smoking out of the same pipe as Alex himself.

This is crazy.

What are the odds?

But Alex did not want to think about odds now, what he wanted was to get high. Higher, at least. But seeing *these* three, it was impossible not to paint lurid thoughts across his imagination. Impossible not to remember tina-fueled fuck-fests, filthy all-nighters, hedonistic orgies. His life consisted of that duality: filthy, drug-driven sex and writing inexplicably successful novels.

How could he ever explain it to any of them? He was sure each of them had been damaged by their prior interactions with him. He was not oblivious. But what was the point in keeping someone around when there were so many other new someones out there to play with? So many other new stories to absorb and spit back out. His success depended on the churn of people through his sex life. There was little other socialization in which Alex still participated.

What's the fucking point? Everyone is just a shell. A hole. A wet dick. I just cut out the bullshit. Take what I want. Use what I need. Then write about it.

Alex could remember being less callous, once. When he had last been in love, and young. When Davis was still a scrawny wet-dream of a boy, not the buffed-out Chelsea queen disconsolately chewing on his fingernails while sitting on Pritchard's bed. Next to fucking Clark Rhondes of all people. Davis had been Alex's first lesson in love, his first success and his most lasting failure. During those sober moments when he was not wholly consumed by his own characters—few and far between though those moments were—when all Alex wanted was to lie motionless in his bed and feel the cool breeze from the window unit roll over him, thoughts of Davis would sometimes surface. Memories of their naive dalliance, their mutual discovery of intimacy, the high which came from being vulnerable and simultaneously full of someone's rigid cock roared through him at those times. Back then, Alex hadn't thought anything else could compare.

I hadn't known about tina then. Or shit, sex, and tina smeared together.

Or the words THE END.

He had been well and truly in love with Davis. And then

he had well and truly fucked it off, as if part of him knew it needed to be fucked off.

I needed to grow beyond fucking Baton Rouge. How could I do that with Davis pulling all my energy into him?

As he swept his eyes around the room again, Alex saw Davis cut his eyes at him while trying not to be seen doing it.

Fucker wants me so bad. He's still in love.

How sad for him.

The sight—the knowledge—did give Alex a mild erection. He loved being wanted. Clark, however—Clarkless, as he apparently called himself now—was pointedly *not* looking at Alex. There had been no love there for Alex, just a fresh-faced, slim-hipped, hairless twink. A twink too stupid to understand he was just a toy, too arrogant to believe he could be toyed with, and too young to understand sex was often just sex and nothing more. Not that Alex had been unhappy abusing Clark, but he always knew there was never going to be more to them than sex. Alex could not keep himself from mentally deriding the kid for not understanding these things.

Grow up kid. No one makes you eat their shit from a dog bowl and actually means it when they say I love you.

In the end it had been simpler to ditch the kid. After all, it wasn't like Clark had been some lonely, pathetic nobody. He had had friends, family, people who loved him dearly. Alex figured it was their job to pick up the shattered, puppy-dog pieces, not his.

Somehow—the why was beyond Alex—it seemed Clark and Davis had gotten close.

More than close. They're fucking into each other. What are they doing? Bumping pussies?

The pair sat very near one another. Too near, in Alex's opinion. As Pritchard prepared a bowl for everyone to smoke, Alex caught Clark narrowing his eyes at Davis's crotch while Davis was busy staring at the newest arrival as though the pretty fucker were a ghost. Davis would catch himself and look back to Clark, sweeping his gaze across Alex himself in the process.

He still wants what he doesn't fucking know he wants. How sad for him.

In a way, the new kid was a ghost. It had been some time since Alex had seen the kid. It took Alex a second before he even recognized the boy, even after Pritchard gave the kid a name. It was shocking that he even remembered the boy at all. Though the kid still looked barely a day over fifteen, his eyes had a hardness about them which was all too grown up: they leered at everything upon which they landed.

The truly startling thing for Alex was that Davis knew the ghost boy. In fact, Alex was sure Davis must have had the boy also. Something in their body language made this implicit: the way Anton leaned in his chair in Davis's direction yet refused to make eye contact with the muscle queen.

Fucking Davis. With muscles. How surreal.

The way Davis would look at Anton, then Clark, then cut his eyes at Alex also spoke to some relationship, some connection between the kid and Davis. Such things were easy to miss, but Alex made a point of noticing such things, had meticulously developed a career around it. His novels consisted of little more than observations of people, taking those details, those minutiae, and crafting a story from them. A story which would eventually, almost miraculously, fit together with the hyperbolic attributes of the characters Alex created.

Success as a novelist had meant many things for Alex: money, comfort, drugs, near endless sex and partying; but the now well-honed ability to quite literally "read" a person was of the most value, as it was the cornerstone of both his success at writing and his success abusing fags.

Alex prided himself on this cornerstone. Occasionally, he would try to share his knowledge with others only to find while he could shape a novel out of those details and have people fawn over it, trying to explain the cogs behind the watching face left people irritated with him. Still, they wanted more. A few even claimed he was patronizing them and being willfully obtuse at the same time. The irony was not lost on Alex. His ability to see clearly into a person—to acutely measure the incongruous pieces and affix them into some kind of artful combination—being seen as blind and patronizing. It was funny to Alex, this lack of understanding from almost everyone in his life, this inability to elucidate his brilliant articulations. To explain what had spurred his flight from Louisiana, from everyone and everything which had been a part of his life.

They just didn't understand me. Why should I have endured that? Why should I spend my life with those hateful spirits?

Especially now that all those fucking pasts are haunting me at once...

Leaving had been much easier than it should have been—even more affirmation that he had been doing the right thing, not that he needed any affirmation. Alex caught Anton staring at him. He stared back. The fucker was *still* wispy and beautiful, Alex had to give him that. And in all his thousands of hook-ups Alex had never met anyone else as naturally inclined to perversion while also as radiantly captivating. Anton had taken to being Alex's abused sex-toy so fast it had partly soured the experience for Alex. He had discovered, in part thanks to Anton, that he *enjoyed* the slow build up, the steady shaving of resolve, until Alex had a boy begging for things which only weeks before would have been vomit-inducing. But that had not been Anton. The kid had begged from the start.

Piss all over me, Sir!

Shit on me, Daddy.

Puke in my mouth, Master!

Flashes of his own father spurred Alex then, given him impetus to abuse Anton the way the kid had wanted to be abused. Alex wanted to laugh as his eyes met Anton's because *it* was still there; the kid's need was plain in the way his head moved to look away. But Alex's eyes held his, the kid couldn't look away. Some stirring of hope inside, no doubt some deluded part of the kid believed the eye contact presaged more, promised more.

Pritchard's arm broke the eye contact as he handed the

bowl to Anton. Well that much had also remained the same: Anton might be desperate to be someone's slave-toy, but he was a slave to tina first. The kid took three huge pulls on the bong before passing it to Clark—in a second hand fashion, as though he wanted to skip the other pretty boy in the room and pass the bong to Davis instead. Twinks were as bad as women about being spiteful with competition. Clark took the bong and hit it three times, offering his mouth to Davis for the last hit, exhaling it directly into Davis's mouth. Alex remembered the first time he had done that. It had been with Davis—one of the first times they had gotten high with each other. But it was different this time. Davis closed his eyes while Clark had his wide open.

Last I heard, Davis was sober... since when does he do shotguns of meth?

Davis and Clark... in love? What kind of gay shit is this?

Davis took his turn but did not offer to exhale for Clark— the twink was lying back on the bed now, too high to notice. Handing the bong to him, Davis's hand brushed Alex's. The corners of Davis's mouth quirked into a minuscule smile. The expression was conspiratorial, as if Davis and Alex were sharing an inside joke at the expense of the others in the room. Alex didn't smile back. He looked instead at Pritchard and nodded in thanks for the tina. Burning the bowl, Alex finished it off, getting four good pulls. He barely felt different—that was standard now. It took shooting up to *really* knock him flat. Still, his body did tingle a bit and his mild erection grew to full hard-on. Alex rubbed it, roughly, over his jeans as he caught Pritchard's eyes, his thoughts plainly written over his face. After Alex handed the bong back, Pritchard refilled it, eager to facilitate the orgy he wanted and saw coming.

Anton spoke, staring at the ground. "Um. I can't stay..." His voice wavered and he sounded unsure.

Probably too high to think. Figures.

"I just needed to buy as much as you've got Pritch and see if you could get Trevie to come deliver the rest..." Pritchard's hand went slack and he set the newly refilled bong down, close to dropping it off the edge of the desk. He look at Anton with open astonishment and slight confusion, head tilted a fraction to the left.

Anton gulped and blinked rapidly—he was sweating now, whether from the tina or the nervousness he was feeling, Alex wasn't sure. "I... came over because I was partyin' with these guys and they wanted to buy some real quantity, but I'm too fucked up to make it to Trevie's and he won't deliver to me, doesn't trust..." The kid's eyes went all shifty as he spoke. Alex wanted to laugh. Whoever this Trevie was, Anton had screwed him over big time."I was hoping you'd help me and take a cut..."

Pritchard's expression was annoyed and bemused, but finally settled on dismissive. "How much are you wanting, Anton, *dear*?" Pritchard said, the condescension inherent in his upturned chin and withering tone.

Anton swallowed again, "I've got eight thousand bucks...

Pritchard coughed in surprise, exhaled a thick snowy breath of tina. "Are you fucking serious? What idiot gave *you* eight thousand dollars?" The words spilled out before Pritchard could stop them, his face recording surprise at his own words.

Anton pulled out a huge wad of cash from his little pack. He shoved it at Pritchard, his angelic face darkened by Pritchard's reaction. Both Pritchard and Clark goggled at the money, but to Alex (and likely Davis as well) it was only impressive when considering the source. Still, it would buy a lot of tina. Alex had been careful in *that* aspect, mostly. His last dealer had gone to prison for dealing tina and Alex wouldn't ever make the mistake of keeping so much tina around at one time.

Never more than two grams at a time and always in one bag.

Alex fought back an urge to leave but then he would not have any tina for himself, not until Pritch could re-up again.

"Well, I'd like my two grams first," Alex said, smiling without showing teeth. Pritchard was still completely taken aback, still not over Anton's huge cash wad. Davis chiming in next did not help.

"Same for me."

Clark nodded, which sealed things for Alex: Davis and Clark were definitely fucking.

Who cares? They're both my cast-offs. If they wanna fuck...

Alex choked back a snarl. The idea of having an orgy did not bother Alex. In fact, he was certain it would be enjoyable— even more so if the four of them ditched Pritchard and went back to Alex's place, where there was a sling, benches, toys, and restraints, and where poppers could be used without

Pritchard's bitching.

And a play room with rubber floors and walls...

This thought soothed Alex. Pritchard was too squeamish to be into what Alex and Davis would want to do to the two twinks. Anton looked expectantly from face to face, mouth moving silently, as though he could not figure out what to say next. The indecision on his smooth features was delicious for Alex.

"But I..." Anton started.

Pritchard motioned him to hold off. "I'll call Trevie and we'll see, OK?" Pritchard said.

Anton's mouth closed. He blushed, nodded.

"In the meantime," Pritchard said, eyes leering at them all, "You boys feel free to do... whatever pleases your dear little cocks."

Davis's head turned first to Alex, probably to gauge his reaction before indicating his own desire. This was no mystery to Alex: *Davis is still in love with me. Fucking moron.* Despite whatever was going on with Clark, who was clearly infatuated with Davis, Davis was inexplicably hung up on Alex, which left Alex with only derision for Davis. Yet he would *jump* at the chance to play with Davis, as long as the two twinks were around to abuse. Even if it meant encouraging Davis's unrequited affections for Alex.

Davis tried to become me because he can't have me. How sad for him.

Clark's eyes narrowed as he watched Davis's attention fixate on Alex. The twink crossed his arms, with obvious sulking displeasure, over his chest. Whatever Anton and Davis felt for Alex, whatever lingering unmet needs still drove them—love for Davis, lust for Anton—Clark clearly did not feel the same way. He had moved on.

To fucking being in love with a basic imitation of ME. Is everyone fucking stupid? Do they all those their minds over this love shit? Can't they see it doesn't work?

Alex quietly sighed.

What the fuck?

Still. Those problems are theirs. Not mine.

Might as well get my rocks off. But I'm going to be in control, whatever Davis thinks.

He stood up and covered the short step between himself and the bed, where his bulging crotch was centered in front of Davis's face. Grabbing the back of the muscle-queen's head, Alex pulled it forcefully towards his crotch. His heart wasn't in it. Davis was far too old for that. Less than a minute later he pulled his wet, still limp cock out of Davis's mouth and slapped him in the face with it. Davis made a sound of guttural, animal pleasure. Alex ignored him, grabbed Anton and shoved the twink towards Alex's ass while he presented his flaccid, moist dick to Clark. Clark's face was glum and his lips were tightly closed. Anton, however, was pulling, greedy, clawing at the back of Alex's jeans, desperate to get them down. Alex pulled Clark's jaw open and pressed his dick into the twink's unwilling mouth before he caught the expression on the rest of Clark's face.

Disgust.

It was something wholly new to Alex. He had never seen *that* expression on the face of someone who held his dick in their mouth. His insides went slack, deflated, and his knees almost gave way. A slow vertigo crept up on Alex and he was tugging at his jeans, pulling them insistently *up* before he even realized what he was doing. Clark moved away, now sitting where Anton had been sitting, arms still crossed over his chest and his look of sullen disgust, taking in the whole room now. Memories of Clark came back to Alex—before he was Clarkless, seventeen and whip-cord slender—lying atop Alex, with Clark's taut stomach facing up, Alex's cock sleeved inside the twink's ass. In the memory, Clark turned his head to the side, levered down his mouth so it was abreast of Alex's ear and whispered, "I never want this to end. I love you."

Alex recalled that moment, not because he had felt the same way Clark did—not even remotely close. He remembered it because it was as if Clark had been locked, shut up tight and held aloof, despite the fact that they had been dating for some time. Despite the fact Alex had fucked, fisted, and pissed on the kid. The kid had still managed to hold himself distant, not truly commit himself to Alex. But that moment had been Clark handing Alex the keys, and the pleasure had been so *heightened* and *pure* Alex had cum and fallen asleep right after, softened cock still inside Clark.

An hour after Clark told Alex he loved him, Alex began to train the boy to accept true abuse. The same way he once trained Davis and would eventually train others. Clark had been far more resistant—harder to bend to the bit—but those words sealed him to Alex and Alex had used them against Clark, again and again.

But now, in Pritchard's studio apartment, the opposite of that moment was staring Alex full in the face. He could not handle it. All he could think to do was run, leave. Shock, mirrored on Davis and Anton's faces, gave way to disappointment as Alex moved towards the door. Pritchard had just finished a hushed conversation on his phone, his semi-flaccid penis peeking out of his leather pants as he casually pulled at it. Pritchard hung up the phone and gave Alex a confused glance as Alex stumbled into his clothes and leaned towards the front door.

"You still want..?" Pritchard said. The overall image of this slightly old man, limp dick dangling between leather-crusted legs, left Alex with a need to laugh even amid his sudden twist of anxiety. But the need was not enough to overwhelm the strange emotion rushing through him from seeing that expression on Clark's face. It was as if all the times Alex had been cavalier with other people's emotions, all the times he had run out, left someone wanting while he himself was full and satiated, chose this moment to strike revenge via Clark's withering stare. His parents and sister's faces were in that expression. All of who he was and had been was there and whether it was real or not did not seem to matter. It was like the Magic Mirror Gate in the Neverending Story, where brave men discovered they were in fact cowards, where the strong found they were actually weak. Where Alex found he was the antithesis of a man aloof, able to take and abuse and waste the

217

hearts of others without consequence to his own. This knowledge held him by the scruff of the neck, shook him, and refused to let go.

Alex managed to catch his breath, not looking at anyone but Pritchard. Emotion raged through him—things he had long thought dealt with, handled, over and done. Despite all of this, the clarion call of the tina, a Siren of violent necessity, remained, overpowering everything else to ensure its song was heard loudest. Fishing out four hundred dollar bills, Alex's shaking, twitching hand set them down on the desk next to Pritchard's bong. Pritchard lifted a pair of small bags full of tina, placed them delicately in Alex's palm.

Alex squeezed the bags tight and ran out of the apartment. He hustled down the stairs, sweaty hands gripping the railing, his unsteady footing nearly causing him to twice fall down. Only his wet grip on the round wooden banister saved him. When he finally made his way out the front door of the building, he was shocked to see it was almost full-on morning. The sun would soon be coming up over the tall buildings of eastern Manhattan. Alex's whole body shook and his mind narrowed, to focus on getting back to his apartment, off the streets and comfortably ensconced in solitude, only a glass pipe and his cat for company. But when he reached the subway stop at Eighth Avenue, a sign informed him the E train was not running. The man behind the plate glass instructed him to catch it on 14th Street.

Swearing to himself as he climbed up the stairs and out of the subway station, Alex speed-walked away, head down, mind checked out from his surroundings. He angled from Eighth Ave., hoping to catch the N in Union Square instead of going all the way to 14th for the E. The streets blurred as he walked—he wove in and out of people's way, paying little attention to any of them. He felt constantly under watch, as though everyone passing were fixated on him with full scrutiny, eyes trained on him, *knowing.* Seeing deeper into him than he could ever hope to see into them, and understanding everything in life which had eluded Alex until then.

Why had the little room of Pritchard's apartment suddenly become something dark and heinous? Something tinged with foreboding and ominousness? There was nothing in that place which Alex had not done before, nothing he had not seen, and no one he had not fucked. So why the vertigo? Why the fear? An answer seemed tantalizingly close, just under the skin of his temples, but when he reached out with his mind to grab it the answer flitted away like smoke rising from a Manhattan manhole.

His phone buzzed, insistent. Reaching into his pocket while he paused on 18th Street and Seventh Avenue, Alex sighed when he saw the message from Pritchard on the phone's display.

Alex. Come Back. ;)

His body shook with implied violence tempered only by doubt and indecision. Alex stared at the phone for a full minute.

Should I go back?

What is there to be afraid of, fuck? I used them all and left them behind! I left THEM. They have nothing over me! No hold, no power. I'm successful, strong, rich... AND beautiful! Who cares if Davis looks like a Greek god now or that fuckin' Anton kid is as pretty as the day I first gagged him with my cock. And Clark...

Alex's heart pinged, reflexively, unprepared for the thoughts of his last real relationship. For the memory of what he had left behind with Clark: the kid had grown up into everything his promise had indicated—he was handsome but not striking, thin and lithe, whip-crack smart, and a functionally balanced hedonist.

Is that the problem?

Alex wondered at his latent feelings for the kid. Had his abrupt departure years back, leaving Clark fully in the lurch— had that left something unfinished within Alex himself? He wanted the idea to be absurd, had built up a confidence in himself over the past years since running away from Louisiana. One which did not include most of how he had felt about himself back then, particularly how he had felt about Clark, and to a lesser extent, Davis. Alex had willfully become a wholly new person, his old life had been molted and left to desiccate. Still, something in him churned and lashed. He could not seem to decide whether to allow his feet to turn back towards Pritchard's apartment, towards the men of his past. Gathered into a greasy pile of flesh, getting high and filthy.

An insight—as terrible and kinetic as the first sight of an electric chair by a condemned man—flashed through Alex. He set his jaw, his decision made, the doubt vanished. Alex retraced his steps back towards Pritchard's. He was still afraid for some reason he could not understand. His body still wanted to shake with the tremors of that fear. His heart raced, his throat was scratchy and raw. He knew his voice would likely crack if he tried speaking. Alex determined to return to Pritchard's anyway.

This is the new me. If I let fear control me then I'm the OLD Alex. And I refuse—REFUSE!—to ever go back to being HIM.

Alex nodded to himself and his silent words.

The blocks ambled past. Alex walked slower than usual, hoping to divine something in the steps, anything, some answer to what was roiling about in his head. But by the time he reached 28th Street there was still nothing more than nascent fear and the tantalizing sensation of an answer just beyond his awareness. That and a steely determination. He kept his head down, not wanting to make eye contact with anyone. Alex was about to push the buzzer to Pritchard's outer door when he stopped, stock-still and frozen.

Am I really going to do this?

They're probably all fucking by now. I can jump in like it's nothing. Just fuckin' piggy sex. Nothing more.

The realization did not turn him on as it should. All the men up there were hot, uninhibited, and into Alex. He had not had the problem of being unable to separate his lust from his emotion since he left Louisiana. His body should have been aching to engage. He should have been rock hard, but he was not. Determination be damned, his hands still trembled.

"Excuse. Me," a deep voice said from behind him. Alex

grunted in surprise and moved away from the door—only a bit, just enough so the man who had spoken could buzz whichever apartment the man wanted to access. The man brushed past towards the panel of buttons. Alex, for a brief moment, forgot all his twisting thoughts as he took in the man's appearance. He was gorgeous: tall, naturally muscular, with unmarred, smooth, light brown skin, and his deep, nearly-black hair was artfully styled with the unkempt precision of a true artist. Alex was instantly sure the man was not gay. Possibly bisexual, or merely metrosexual, maybe, but not gay. Something in the man's posture made that obvious. The man smiled, his perfect white teeth gleamed as he reached over and buzzed apartment 2B.

Pritchard's apartment?

This guy knows Pritchard?

Maybe he IS gay?

Alex goggled before he spoke. His heart pounded, throat ready to catch, Alex's voice cracked. He had to swallow several times, blanch, and repeat himself.

"You're—you're... You're here to see Pritchard?" Alex said.

The man's eyes widened—a bit, not much—and after giving Alex a careful up-and-down look the man nodded.

"Yes."

Alex returned the nod, "Me too." He could not help himself. Alex grinned, lasciviously.

Is THIS why Pritchard called me to come back?

Alex understood that, maybe. Pritchard might have known this man was Alex's type, as far as non-twinks went. Perhaps

222

Pritchard had sent the others away and wanted to play with Alex and this man. He raised eyebrows at the man, waiting for him to introduce himself. When he did not, Alex smiled harder, wider, his *most* winning smile, coming right on the heels of his *most* lusty grin, none of which phased the man.

"I'm Alex," Alex said, extending his hand. He barely managed to keep from shaking with a combination of fear and excitement. The man took Alex's hand—the textured skin on his palm and fingers was rough, his hand was heavily calloused, if thin-fingered.

"Prather," the man said. The buzzer went off, the front door maglock was unlocked. Prather hesitated and, instead of going in first, opened the door for Alex. Alex used the moment to adjust himself so his hard-on would be obvious.

There's no point in being subtle when it comes to sex.

Alex walked up the stairs, not turning back to see if Prather followed. He did not need to—he heard the man following behind him. At the top of the second landing there was Pritchard's door, half-open. A fully naked Pritchard, his signature leather chaps inexplicably gone, leaned out from behind that door, a very, very slick smile on his face.

"You came back!" Pritchard said through his smile, his tone thick with peppery disbelief.

Alex sighed, went inside, gently pushing Pritchard aside to do so. Prather followed close behind. "You must be Prather?" Pritchard asked excitedly, his tone making his admiration of Prather's beauty obvious.

"Pritchard?" Prather questioned.

"Yes, yes. Come in."

The dark, shelved walls of Pritchard's tiny living room leaned in. Alex saw the look of surprise on the faces of his ghosts, all of whom were now tangled up on the bed, naked.

Was I gone that long?

They were already sweaty and greasy. Clark and Davis with art-deco hard-ons while Anton lay between them with obvious crystal dick. Alex realized the look of surprise on Anton's face was not directed at him, but at the man who had come up with him. *Prather.* Alex turned to look at Prather and saw the man was as shocked, or nearly so, as Anton.

"Anton. Have you spoken to your mother?" Despite the implication of concern in his words, Alex heard nothing of actual concern in Prather's tone. *Like he doesn't give any fucks.* Prather sounded calmly blasé. Anton gaped, a mild something suffused those bright, white, grease-streaked cheeks with heat.

"I... I've been busy," Anton said and looked away.

"Well, you should call her and let her know you're OK. That's most of what she wants." Again, though his words implied a scolding, his tone carried none. Anton looked away, sweat dripping off him. Davis and Clark pressed against him like homoerotic bookends.

Pritchard slid into his computer chair—a pleased look on his face. "I'm *so* glad you came back Alex, dear." Pritchard snickered. "We all did a shot and I decided I would like to make a porno. I hoped... Well, I hoped you'd be willing to be the dom-top. You could be obscured, of course." Pritchard

224

lifted up a rubber mask and dangled it at Alex like a grandfather presenting a known and well-loved toy.

What? A fucking porno?

Alex had made porn before – never with Pritchard though –but Alex had always insisted on wearing a mask of some kind.

How would Pritchard know that?

Pritchard isn't into the truly filthy stuff. His limits don't go much past fisting and bondage. What is he up to? Alex turned to Prather, who seemed deeply unaffected. Pritchard noticed Prather and he said, "Oh. Yes, dear me. Did you get, I mean, do you have it?" Prather nodded and pulled out a large plastic sack, bulging with huge shards of tina. He handed the sack over to Pritchard.

Anton saw the sack and sat bolt upright, his forehead pushing Davis's slick cock aside as he sat up. The twink's eyes widened at the amount of drugs in the sack. He licked his lips.

"Trevie said to hold on to the money. He will get it from you later."

Pritchard nodded.

Alex shuddered, leaned into a turn towards leaving.

Why did I come back here?

His earlier fear came back, amplified by the sight of so much tina. If he was caught around so much, it would mean years and years in prison and the end of his high-flying career as a novelist. Alex looked over at the bed, where Anton wriggled away from the others, the spots of grease on him complicating matters. The twink had such a look of obvious determination that Alex found himself momentarily compelled momentarily by it, dick pressing hard against his jeans in response. Clark and Davis gave mimicked shrugs and went back to touching and exploring each other. Anton rose up off the bed, naked and dripping, and took the sack from Pritchard, almost dropping it from his greasy hands. He pulled on his clothes, tucked the plastic sack of tina inside his little backpack, and made for door, no one paying much attention to him, save Alex and Prather.

Prather said to Anton, "Call Taty." He turned to Pritchard. "Enjoy yourself, Pritchard."

He made to leave.

"Wait!" Pritchard called out, "Why don't you...um, join us, dear man?"

Prather, vigorously—perhaps too much so, shook his head. "I'm sorry, I can't. I have someone with whom I need to meet up."

"Well, Prather dear, it was *very* nice to meet you," Pritchard said, before forgetting the beautiful man in favor of another hit of tina from the bong.

Davis disengaged at the sound of the man's name, looked at Prather, eyes narrowed with sudden recognition. "Wow," Davis mumbled, "it's you."

"Davis?" Prather said.

Davis grinned at him. "I was totally hoping to fuck you." Prather nodded as if that were a normal comment, and more, as if he had already been completely aware of the fact. Davis's grin slipped but did not fall away.

"I don't think that would be fair to Jules," Prather responded.

Didn't Davis have a fag hag named Jules?

Alex goggled at the mention of Jules, but Davis more so. "I thought you dumped her...?" Davis said.

Prather nodded. "I did. But I made a mistake. I intend to go remedy that mistake. *Now.*" Davis looked torn between happiness and resentment, which for Alex seemed a perfect summation of man. Only then did Alex fully recall the name Jules. Not just a hag, but Davis's best friend: a loud, insistent gadfly, fun in a social sense, but high-strung and irritating. She was everything Alex disliked about women. Of course, this made him think of Annette. But he pushed that away before it could grow into something else entirely, some paroxysm worse than the one in which he was already embroiled. Annette was one ghost Alex was not *ever* going to let come back. Like the sense of vertigo he had experienced earlier, a rush of understanding came to him.

Jules dating this Prather? How fucking unreal is that? Wasn't she a frumpy, emotional wreck who only had her social skills as a form of compensation for her withering self-doubt? And somehow this same Prather knows Anton, Davis, and Pritchard? What the holy fuck is happening?

It was like the whole of the world Alex had built for himself in New York—the intoxicating newness of the City still with him even after years—was poisoned by the remains of his old life, and Alex had not seen it coming. But it pressed him now on all sides, like a vise. How was it possible for these

227

intersecting lines to occur between these people? New York was supposed to be *too big* for such things, a primary draw of the place for Alex. Being a stranger among strangers had been a huge part of the sexy allure which made New York so amazing. At that moment, however, the very words New York City felt like loaded words, unmet promises of faithfulness, emptied of all worth.

"I... I can't fucking do this," Alex said low. Heads turned towards him and he looked away, afraid he would get choked up. His hands shook, sweaty again. Anton hovered towards the door, his face locked on Alex in the midst of some obvious and dire indecision. Alex backed away. Davis hid disappointment behind a mocking leer, which Alex could read between the brief, desultory glances. Clark paid Alex no mind at all, and Pritchard shook his head sadly. Alex edged further off until his back was to the door.

Davis caught Alex's eyes and held them. A quiet fire laced the blueness of Davis's irises, undiminished by the wildness of the rest of his slick, greased appearance; the man's eyes were serene, somehow. Alex chafed with unknown feelings, wondered what his own eyes betrayed.

I'm a writer, I'm supposed to know my own feelings...

As he looked at Davis, he knew something remained unmet between them. It lingered, binding them, however tenuously. It was not quite regret and nowhere near love, but somewhere between the two. A new word needed to be created to define how Alex felt, some grand, amazing crush of sentiments and cleverness, a word which could explain itself in context and live on.

Like the word delicious. Or frisson.

I don't know... Maybe I can create it.

Am I not a master of words?

Alex's whole life had been an attempt at being a master of words. From the invented stories he would act out in his backyard, to those he would concoct to hide his faggotry from his doting mother, to the entire life (and the second, secret life) he had constructed in New York: the new autobiography of a successful writer. He felt the lack keenly, this loss for how to describe what he felt. *Is this what I strove to become?* He shook the thought away angrily and broke eye contact with Davis.

Years before, Alex had willfully broken himself into two pieces, one which held most of him: his experiences, eloquence, some of his passions and his perversity. The other piece he shoveled full of his past loves: family, hometown, and insecurities. He had left the latter piece on the parqueted kitchen floor of a cheap apartment, bolted the door behind, and left it to starve. Only now he realized it hadn't died. It grew while Alex was not paying attention, tentacles lengthening across the years until they came back and touched everything, their need like suckers which would never release. Staring at Davis, Alex saw a sex-fueled incarnation of the same, starved beast he had tried to diligently to discard—no longer pathetic and abandoned, but fully grown and rapacious. And out for his blood.

There was love there, still. A resonance of like to like, of self to self. As surely as Alex despised that part of himself, he loved it as well, and he saw the slant rhyme in Davis, a depraved monster of Alex's own making. Unable to process what he felt, Alex choked back a sob and rushed out of Pritchard's apartment, thoughts scattered, his feet on autopilot. The primal thought of *away* drove him onward. 28th St. rushed by. Seventh Ave. came to Sixth Ave. When he reached Park a sudden feel for the direction he traveled emerged, and he turned south. Walking briskly—paying little attention to the surroundings, the mass of people in the New York morning going about their separated business—Alex pushed past street after street, hardly noticing when he offended someone or pushed too hard. Until someone pushed back.

"Son?" the voice said, so familiar, so dead.

So unwelcome.

Only it was not dead. The voice was alive, like it had been all those years ago. When Alex had been different...

"PRESS, son!" Dad barked. Alex pushed his legs as hard as he could, tried to bear his shoulder into the rack of pads meant to approximate a defensive lineman. Alex was a tall, lanky kid of 11 years—dour, fanciful, and knowingly strange. But here, in this football uniform and the accompanying pads, his shoulders exaggerated madly, his thoughts encased and limited by a helmet, his grunts silenced behind a mouthpiece—he was something different, something strong and male. Something Dad could finally be proud of. Churning up little divots of turf underneath his spiked cleats, Alex's legs pumped. Slowly, the metal contraption of padding

and weights began to move.

"That's it, son! PRESS! That's my boy!"

Alex's legs gave out. His ankle twisted and he cried out in a girlish shriek, a high-pitched sound, piercing and shrill. Even as he fell, his eyes sought Dad's, locked onto them. Alex, even then, had needs too strong for him to resist. Dad's acceptance, his brutal affection, his disdain: they were all part of what Alex fed upon. Before Dad could correct him, Alex saw what he expected, what he needed and hated to need: contempt, mockery, cruelty. Though Alex did not yet have those words, he knew their meanings all too well. Alex saw the disdain in the cut of his father's quivering jaw, and his cries cut off soon after he hit the grass. Seconds later, when Dad wrenched himself from the football contraption and rushed over to check on him, Alex bunched in on himself, his pads making it look comical and slightly painful. He shied away from his Dad, full of shame at both his humiliation and the weird, discordant sense that he wanted more of it.

"I'm OK." Alex sniveled, unable to wipe his nose through the helmet, refusing to make further eye contact. Dad helped him up despite Alex's best attempts to keep shying away. Dad released him.

"Take the bench, Alex."

And with that, the part of Alex which would unmoor itself one day and grow larger than any destiny to which Alex was entitled— snapped into being. It pressed itself up and out of the deep dark within Alex, blinked, snarling and pissed off at the Sun above even as it ached for the heat of its touch...

"S-s-son? Is it really you?" his Dad said. Alex looked up

and shied away from the sight before him. Ray Richardson's mustache was still there, only now it was sprinkled with silver. His father's face was far more lined than Alex remembered: wrinkled and spattered with age, cares, troubles, and crevices of disappointment. Even his lips seemed old, withered. Yet none of that was what threw Alex. Beyond the mere presence of his father and that hideous, outdated mustache, Ray Richardson was wearing a wig, a skirt, a blouse—and a fucking pair of clunky heels which made him, for the first time since Alex was a teenager, taller than Alex himself.

After all the years the man had oppressed and persecuted Alex for being gay and weak and so many other things, after all the years Alex had oppressed himself in some sick, sycophantic pantomime of Ray Richardson's false machismo, here the man was, looming over Alex, his sad, maudlin drag a mockery of Alex's own personhood. And a cheap, gaudy, second-hand mockery at best. Yet there was a difference Alex could immediately discern from the last time he had seen his father, years before.

When Dad dropped the cross-dressing bomb on their family, Alex had not been there. It had not been a bomb to Alex, who knew for years that Ray Richardson hid things about himself, though Ray had not known Alex knew. But his Dad admitting to the cross-dressing and bisexuality openly, *that* had been explosive. Even when Alex's sister told him over the phone and Alex was forced to pretend like it was a complete, shocking surprise. After that moment, Alex refused to see any of them again in person, strangely unmoved by the sound of his mother bawling in the background, likely as she contemplated the shambles Ray Richardson had made of her life.

I understand that pain, Mom. I really fucking do, Alex thought, even as he hung up the phone and steeled himself to leave them all behind.

The difference in his father was that Dad no longer looked like Alex's mom in bad, sad drag, as he looked in the photos Alex had found on his father's old 486 IBM PC. Someone had been at Ray Richardson, had improved him so he now looked more like a blowsy woman of 1984 than one of 1974.

Alex noticed his Dad was not alone. A woman was attached to his arm. And this woman was most definitely not his Mom.

"Dad?" Alex managed to croak out. Vertigo assaulted him again. His Dad's voice—traveling across years and years—came back, full of unmet expectation, faulty hopes, and dick-scraping letdowns. The voice insistently coaching, full of empty vigor, as Dad always had been, always without being fully present, never delving beyond shouted commands. Ray Richardson had never seemed to wonder what drove his only son, what ticked behind the boy's hurt expression or the feminine cock of his hand perched on his hip as he chewed his lip and looked with anxiety at the other boys.

"PRESS, SON!" Dad's voice commanded.

"PRESS, Son!" Dad's voice echoed.

"Press, Son..." Dad's voice faded.

233

Alex took in the woman on Dad's arm. She was *large,* if not as much as she had once been. Her skin folds were artfully concealed beneath expensive plus-size wear, and her neck displayed the marks of a tendency to over-eat. Her hair was loose and beautifully kept, which mitigated the shape of her body to some degree. With her free hand she trailed her finger —delicately painted a pretty shade of mauve, another checkmark in Alex's plus column—through her sleek, dark brown hair. Alex caught a full glimpse of her face and she gave him a skittish smile before looking towards Dad. Her hand, done with her hair, fidgeted at her side.

"I can't believe we ran into you, Son! I just saw your ex, that Davis, a few days ago. I hoped... I really did... but I never expected I'd see you... like this..."

Alex looked at Dad again and closed his eyes rather than see the looks plain on his father's face: hope, need, pride. *How dare the man have pride now?* It was as though a circle had closed around Alex Richardson, ringed by his ghosts, like some inverse parody of Harry Potter at the end of the Goblet of Fire. Those ghosts hand in hand and chanting in some foreign language, words coarse and guttural but spoken with delight and urgent, malicious need. Hoping to silence the ghosts, Alex repeated his own chant, like a mantra.

I left this behind. I am not him. Not anymore. Never again...
I left this behind. I am not him. Not anymore. Never again...

Alex's fists balled up, his stomach clenched, and his jaw grew tight, as though he were about to attempt a heavy squat at the gym. He opened his eyes and took in the misty

234

expression on Dad's face, as well as the worry and excitement on the face of the frumpy woman with Dad. The woman whose arm was wrapped up with Ray's, who had accepted Dad, even with his cross-dressing and bisexuality.

That fucking DICK. Cross-dressing? Bisexuality? And he's inflicting that shit on this poor, sad old woman? REALLY?

"I won't do this," Alex said through hard-bitten teeth, his voice sharp and mean. Determination pressed him into something new, something harder, something which could be reduced no further.

Dad half-smiled as though it were all a joke.

Asshole.

A stern look crossed Dad's face. *Likely preparing to lecture me and maybe hating himself a little for the desire.* The woman looked away. Alex breathed in deep, inhaling the fetid New York morning air. Behind him steam rose from a random manhole. He made to move around Ray, as though the man who had been Dad was now an ill-placed stranger, an obstruction. Alex kept his gaze forward, his neck tight, his resolve hardening with each step.

Union Square opened before him. The park rose up from the buildings surrounding it, the trees backlit by the morning sun, green with life, green with envy. Alex did not look back, didn't allow himself to hear if Ray called after him. He walked past it all, refused to give in to the glory of letting go. Instead he focused his mind on words he did not have, on the hope he could find them if only he pressed forward.

THE END

www.ingramcontent.com/pod-product-compliance
Lightning Source LLC
Chambersburg PA
CBHW060136130626
46556CB00006B/2363